THE SECOND CHANCE PLAN

LAUREN BLAKELY

LAUREN BLAKELY BOOKS

ABOUT

I have a big plan for my career and it most certainly doesn't involve my ex. AKA my first love.

It definitely doesn't entail working with him every day on a brand-new project for my jewelry line.

And it absolutely doesn't include falling for the man all over again.

But the trouble is, he's kind, charming and so damn smart. Not to mention easy on the eyes. And thoughtful, too.

Also, he wants to get to know me again. To take me out for coffee, to chat on the phone, to go to museums.

It's a dizzying, delicious courtship, but I don't know if my heart can handle this from the man who broke it to pieces once upon a time…

Or am I willing to risk everything for a second chance at first love?

This book is for the readers.
For all of you—the lovers
of words and romance.

THE SECOND CHANCE PLAN

By Lauren Blakely

To be the first to find out when all of my upcoming books go live click here!

PRO TIP: Add lauren@laurenblakely.com to your contacts before signing up to make sure the emails go to your inbox!

Did you know this book is also available in audio and paperback on all major retailers? Go to my website for links!

PROLOGUE

Bryan

Five Years Ago

There's no such thing as love at first sight.

I've felt a lot of things after one glance at a beautiful girl, but none of them were love. Love isn't about how someone looks, and what can you know about a stranger when your eyes meet across a crowded room?

That she was beautiful in every single way, from her dark, wavy hair to her gorgeous brown eyes to the soft curves of her body?

All true, but not the reason I fell so hard for Kat Harper.

It was the coffee, the movies, the laughter. It was long conversations, slow walks through the small town, and starry nights on the beach with the waves rolling in. When I held her hand, I felt the start of something, and possibilities unfurled like a red carpet leading the way to her. When I held her hand, the world would melt away, leaving only the two of us.

Only, it wasn't just the two of us.

More like the three of us.

Kat, me . . . and the most complicated third party of all-*time*.

Because love doesn't always show up when you're ready for it.

Sometimes there's too much life in the way.

Fortunately, I didn't believe in love at first sight.

*Un*fortunately, that didn't seem to matter.

1

KAT

Present Day

He was my first favorite mistake.

I hadn't seen him in five years, and as he walked to the front of the classroom, my every muscle tensed, and my brain spun into hyperdrive. What was he *doing* here? Was he in the wrong classroom? Was I?

Professor Oliver was at the front of the room in his customary three-piece suit, spectacles, and a silk handkerchief, and scrawled on one of the white-boards in blue marker was the name of the class: Experiential Learning.

So I was where I was supposed to be—in the front row of desks in my grad school class, learning a new definition for the word "unfair."

Be strong. Be cool. Be badass.

Don't think of lights going down in movie theaters, or of

hot summer nights, miles away from here, tangled up in him.

Too late. I cataloged every detail, from the slightest trace of stubble on his jawline to the way his brown hair invited fingers to run through those waves to how the checkered navy-blue shirt he wore had probably never looked quite so good as when it hugged his arms and stretched across his chest.

I ran my index finger across the silver charm on my necklace. I'd made it when I left for college with the notion that the miniature movie camera could channel steely resolve into me, and I'd needed it these last few years.

At the head of the classroom were other business school alums who would serve as mentors for my fellow grad students this term. Bryan joined them, turned, and froze when he saw me.

Somehow, I'd never considered he might be one of the mentors for this class, even though I knew he was a notable alum. I was over him, and he didn't automatically come to mind. Only occasionally, when I walked around campus and remembered touring the grounds together that summer before he started business school here, how we'd walked arm in arm, making plans. Making promises.

How that had been the last time I'd seen him before he broke my heart and became the first charm on my necklace—the inspiration for my jewelry.

Now, his green eyes locked with mine for the briefest of moments. Maybe it was my imagination, but I thought I saw a tinge of regret in them. If there was, he recovered a second later, and flashed a quick, closed-mouth smile to the class.

Oh. Naturally, it wouldn't bother him to see me here. He didn't care about me then. Why should he care what I thought now?

And the reverse was true too.

Professor Oliver was his usual peppy self as he introduced the mentors. One of the women ran a venture fund she'd started herself; another had been a superstar skateboarder then launched a line of skatewear that was now hugely popular with teens. One of the guys oversaw a firm that had designed some of the most successful iPhone apps, and another founded a health video service.

The fifth was Bryan Leighton—five years older than I was, and I already knew what he did for a living. I knew other things about him too. I knew what his lips tasted like. How his arms felt when I skimmed my palms over the muscles there. How his kisses went on and on, how I never wanted them to end.

Then, like a hypnotist had snapped their fingers, I was back in time. Not yet a graduate student, not yet in the first row of the classroom, just a girl fresh from high school graduation, wrapped around her brother's best friend. Bryan ran his hands through my hair, kissing my neck, and I shuddered. Everyone else, everything else, faded away.

The memory was a trap. A carnivorous plant like

the ones that kept their prey high on sticky and sweet
nectar while they slowly drank them up. I could have
stayed trapped like that, stuck to the memory of the
way his touch thrilled, the promises we'd whispered . .
.

I gripped the charm and, with it, felt how much it
had hurt that he'd broken up with me on the flimsiest
of rationales. I needed that spark of latent anger to
break away from the past. There was no room for the
memory of Bryan Leighton in my life. I needed to stay
sharp and focus on the present.

That lovestruck teenager was gone. I was a capable
twenty-three-year-old woman. I'd already earned my
bachelor's degree from NYU and was finishing my
master's degree from the same school, building a
business, and paying the rent in a Chelsea apartment,
which was no small thing.

Besides, there was only a one-in-five chance I'd be
paired with him. It made much more sense for the
professor to match me with the skate-wear gal, since
we were both in the fashion business. I was a jewelry
designer after all, with a line of necklaces already
selling well online and in several boutiques around
the city.

Professor Oliver rocked back and forth on his
wingtips, seeming to relish the process of pairing off
students with mentors. He read the first student name
from the list, who he assigned to iPhone guy. Okay, so
twenty-five percent chance I'd match with Bryan
now. I crossed my fingers. Next came the venture-

fund woman, partnered off with the student on the end of the row.

One-in-three chance now. I mentally crossed my fingers and toes. Professor Oliver read the names of another student and the health-video-service guy.

That was okay. The skateboard gal was still in the running, and we'd make a logical pairing. I could learn so much from someone who'd developed a successful brand in boutique fashion. She looked cool and hip too, with cat's-eye glasses and pink streaks in her black hair.

Professor Oliver said her name, and I held my breath . . .

And had it knocked out of me, my stomach tightening and my heart sinking, when he called on someone else.

"And that means, Ms. Harper, that your business mentor for this semester will be Bryan Leighton."

Of all the classrooms in all the towns in all the world . .

.

Since I couldn't hunch over a stiff drink like Bogie, and all the other students were getting up to shake hands with their assigned mentors, I dragged myself out of my seat, smoothed my blouse, and did the same. Our paths intersected just in front of Professor Oliver, who beamed at us.

"Excellent. I'm sure you'll have a very productive term. Now, allow me to officially introduce you two."

Bryan held out his hand as if he'd didn't remember me, when I knew he did—I'd seen it on his face. A face that was now sociably neutral.

"A pleasure, Ms. Harper," he said by rote, as if he'd never met me, never touched me.

"All mine," I said just as blandly, wishing that weren't a little bit true.

2

KAT

Present Day

I had been looking forward to this class since I applied to New York University's Stern School of Business. After today, we'd spend the rest of the semester dealing with real businesses, tackling real issues, and gaining insight into how to make our fledgling ventures fly.

This was far more than an academic project for me though. When I was nineteen, a boutique owner in my hometown had stopped me to ask where I'd gotten my charm necklace. She'd called it unusual and eye-catching, and I'd proudly told her I'd made it myself, and that had been the start of my plan. I realized then that I wanted to be a business owner, not a designer working for someone else's brand, which meant I'd have to learn the ins and outs of building a business.

I'd never told anyone but my best friend, Jill, what had inspired the charms that caught on with buyers. Each person found their own meaning in them, so no one had to know that they began as my way of taking something back after Bryan's callous brush-off. If I could sing, maybe I'd have Taylor Swifted him into a girl-power anthem and made a video with my squad. One with a lot of cathartic explosions.

Eventually, though, I didn't want to think "Screw you, Bryan Leighton" every time I put on one of my designs, but I kept the "My Favorite Mistake" theme because I liked the idea of turning ugly rejection and hurt into something special and beautiful.

The boutique owner had started carrying my necklaces and the "My Favorite Mistakes" brand had become a customer favorite in her store, and soon at my parents' shop too, then at others in Manhattan. The trouble was I made all the charms by hand, and the bespoke nature was getting a little challenging. I needed practical skills, and I wanted to learn them from someone who knew how to make a success of a new business.

But I wasn't only about my success. My parents ran a little gift shop in the tourist town of Mystic, Connecticut, where they'd had a hard time of it during the economic downturn a few years back. They'd taken out a loan to keep inventory stocked, and I hated to see them struggling to keep up payments. The store was their nest egg, their key to eventual retirement. They'd worked hard my whole life—putting my brother and me through college, weathering financial storms and health troubles. Now, they were within spitting distance of retirement, and I wanted to make sure they could enjoy some well-deserved time off. I'd taken out loans to pay for business school, but they weren't due for several years. The quicker my own business ramped up, the quicker I'd be able to help pay off the loan on theirs.

Was it too much for me to ask to learn in a distraction-free zone? Working alongside the man who'd broken my heart was not conducive to focus or flow. Especially not when Bryan looked even better than before. In his early twenties, he'd had a sweet, boyish face. Now, he was twenty-eight, and his features were more refined. After five years of running a corporation, he was more sophisticated—his style, his clothes, even the way he carried himself. He'd definitely kept in shape, even with an office job. His tailored shirt hinted at toned muscles, and his handshake had gripped me as inescapably as his forest-green eyes.

The small classroom hummed with the sound of the other students and mentors chatting. I glanced over at where Professor Oliver went around, cheerfully introducing or checking in with the pairs. He seemed invested in everyone getting along and working together—he was hard not to like, actually. Maybe I should at least try to make things work before I messed up his matchmaking.

As I took the seat next to Bryan, I donned my armor and pictured my mom. She'd met everything, from a devastating car accident to the long recovery to the financial hardships that followed, with a tough kind of optimism, brushing one palm against the other and saying, "Let's get to work."

So that's what I was going to do.

"This was my favorite class when I went here," Bryan said, breaking the silence.

"Oh?" I was intently focused on . . . focusing.

He cleared his throat, sounding awkward. "You're right. I suppose it's not really a class," he amended.

I looked at him in surprise—Was he nervous?—and a little confusion. "Did I say it wasn't a class?"

"I inferred it from this"—he pointed, from a safe distance, to the knot between my brows—"thing you have going on here."

Perfect. Now *I* felt awkward as I relaxed my forehead and smoothed the furrow with my finger. "Are you saying that I have a resting bitch face?"

His mouth opened soundlessly, and his eyes widened. "I would never. I can't even imagine what that would look like on you. Which was why I thought you disagreed with my word choice."

My exhale was more a scoff than a laugh. "Trust me—if you see my bitch face, it won't have anything to do with what to call this . . ." I gestured to the room and its occupants, all seeming to be further along with their plans than we were.

He winced—and he ought to—and looked even more awkward and nervous than before, and he didn't hurry to fill the silence. I gave in first.

"What do we call it, then?" I asked, turning to him expectantly. "If it's not a class."

Turning the question over, he mused, "It's not strictly an internship. Not a practicum or a symposium. Maybe 'fieldwork'?"

"That sounds like we'll need test tubes and sample collecting . . . stuff."

"Good point," he said. "And there are places in the city where I wouldn't want to collect samples without a full hazmat suit."

"Best avoided." I kept it deadpan. He was trying to smooth over the past, but I wasn't ready for that, no matter how hard he worked at it. And I'd give him that—he was working pretty hard.

"A workshop?" he suggested. "At least you'd have a birdhouse by the end of it."

How was I not going to ask? "A birdhouse?"

He flashed the lopsided smile I remembered, showing off straight white teeth. "Doesn't everyone build a birdhouse in shop?"

"I wouldn't know. I was in AV club."

"Of course." The smile became a grin, with a *we have an inside joke* chuckle. "You would be, the way you love movies."

If this *were* a movie, there'd be a screeching tire sound effect as he realized his mistake, referencing our awkward—and painful, on my part—past. I could see him mentally searching for the undo button, but it was no good—the tiny bit of thaw I'd felt froze back up, more solid than ever.

I wrapped my hand around the camera charm on my necklace for strength. I couldn't do this. I couldn't start with the smiles and the banter and the teasing that had carried us through that summer in Mystic. One hit and I'd be hooked again, and he'd be in the wind like before.

This wasn't going to work. I couldn't waste this semester or this class . . . workshop . . . seminar . . . whatever. Not only did I need it to graduate, I needed this experience not only for my business but also security for my parents and the shop. I had to absorb as much as I could from my mentor. I couldn't spend all my mental energy second-guessing everything he said or I felt.

I would request a reassignment. Professor Oliver kept office hours, and I would be there like a vulture waiting for him to open his door.

Bryan glanced over at the professor, but when he turned back, he locked his eyes with me, then lowered his voice. "Look, Kat. I had no idea."

"No idea what?" I asked with a side-eye. He could mean a number of things. *I didn't know I'd break your heart. I didn't realize I could be so cruel.*

"When I agreed to be a mentor, I didn't know you'd be in this class."

He held my gaze, and I believed he was sincere. Nothing seemed false. But more than that, I could feel it in the way my stomach fluttered and my heart sped up the longer I stared into his dark-green eyes.

Besides, I had seen his surprise when he caught sight of me. Was he as unhappy about the situation as I was?

"Am I supposed to be grateful that you didn't set this up on purpose?" I couldn't let on that a part of me wished he had. "I'm sorry if this is *awkward* for you, Bryan."

"That's not . . ." He broke off with a shake of his head and reached out as if he was about to touch my arm. But instead, he laced his fingers together on the tabletop and took a long pause to consider his words. Then, in a low, smoky voice, he said, "What I was going to say is . . . I'm glad you are here. I'm glad it worked out this way."

My heart jumped, and I couldn't say which way. There was heat and softening defenses in one direction and bristling, fearful anger in the other. In the middle was confusion and indecision.

I'd spent the last five years moving past my first big love, juggling classes, making jewelry, and building my business.

I would be a fool to jump back into the fire that had already burned me once.

Time was up shortly after that, and I nearly bolted from the classroom and made a beeline for the ladies' room, where I twisted my hair up out of the way with a clip then splashed some water onto my face and tried to get some perspective. And if I happened to give Bryan time to clear the building, even better.

I added some lip gloss so I looked more pulled together than I felt, tucked a strand of dark hair behind my ear, then ventured to the door and peered out into the empty hall. Whew.

The heels of my boots echoed in the wide hallway as I pulled out my phone and tapped the number for my parents' shop. I needed to root myself in the realities of my life—my parents, my plans for them, my goals for the business.

"Mystic Landing. How may I help you?" Mom's voice already made me feel steadier, more grounded.

"Hey, Mom."

"Hey, sweetie!" She dove right in with her usual inquisition. "How are you? How's school? How's Jill? How is My Favorite Mistakes?"

"I'm great. School is fine. I've never had a better roommate. And I'm working hard on the business. But how are you? What's going on with you and Dad and the shop?"

I pictured her waving my question away like so much fluff as she shared a smile with a customer walking into the store. At least, I hoped there were plenty of customers.

"Everything is just fine. A young woman even came in this morning and tried on one of your necklaces."

"Awesome. Did she buy it?"

"No, but she said she'd come back tomorrow."

I tried not to sigh aloud. That usually translated into no sale. "So, are you still getting plenty of late-summer tourists?"

"Oh sure. Of course," she said quickly. Too quickly to trust she wasn't putting on a front so I wouldn't worry, so I followed up with another question.

"What have you been up to today?"

"I rearranged some of the window displays."

My heart sank. That meant she'd had time on her hands. If there were customers, she'd be at the cash register, working the counter, ringing up sundries and gifts for the tourists who streamed in.

She'd be standing at the very same counter where, five years ago, Bryan asked me out on our first date.

I needed blinders to keep in my lane. But would they work if the distraction came from my own mind?

Mom and I talked more about her day, then I told her I loved her and said goodbye.

As I left the building, I nearly dropped my phone when I saw Bryan waiting for me.

It wasn't fair.

How many times after he left me had I wished to see this exact picture?

Now that I sort of semi had things rolling in the right direction, I got my wish. And it threatened to knock me right off course.

3

BRYAN

Five Years Ago

Bruce Springsteen rattled through the speakers of Nate's car as the sun beat down hard through the windshield. "Our last weeks of freedom!" Nate yelled over the music. "We've got to make the most of it. The Boss would want us to."

He'd been my roommate throughout most of college at NYU and then during the MBA program. I had a pretty good read by now when he was just making noise. "Hate to break it to you," I shouted back, "but if you're planning a two-week party, we should have gone to Mexico or something. Not to your parents' house to run their store."

Nate laughed and turned down the stereo as we got into town. "Okay, fine. You got me on that."

"Sounds like they really need this break though," I said. His folks ran a little gift shop and were trusting two newly minted MBAs to keep Mystic Landing running smoothly.

"Well, they put me through school with the shop. And now it's Kat who's headed to NYU in the fall."

Nate had told me plenty about her, to the degree that any guy talks about his sister. I'd seen her picture on Facebook and on his phone, but I'd never given her a second thought. But that changed within minutes of pulling up in his driveway.

Then Kat became all I could think about.

She flung open the door to the house and ran out to launch herself at Nate, wrapping him in a huge hug.

It was not okay for Nate to have a sister this beautiful.

Her pictures didn't do her justice. I didn't know what would. She was the kind of pretty that was impossible to capture.

"I missed you, you big knucklehead," she was telling Nate with a laugh.

"Don't worry. You'll have plenty of time to get sick of me," he said, hugging her back. "You having a good last summer before college starts?"

"The best," she said, then turned to me as I climbed out of the car.

Her dark-brown eyes met and held mine, and I swear I could feel time slow down, full of the heady possibility of a spark.

Then she glanced away, trying not to look at me. The thought that she might feel this too nearly knocked me out.

She wore a light-blue T-shirt, jean shorts, and flip-flops. She was an Ivory Soap kind of girl who didn't need makeup, who could roll out of bed gorgeous because it was all her—the way her eyes sparkled and her smile lit up a . . . well, in this case, a driveway.

"Bryan, this is my sister, Kat."

I set down my duffel bag and extended a hand, quickly realizing she wasn't a handshake kind of girl. So I wrapped her in a friendly hug. She smelled like oranges and sunshine, and the metal of her necklace pendant pressed against my chest.

"I feel like I know you already," I said when I pulled back, and kept to a safe, friendly topic. "Nate says you're a huge movie fan, when you're not making necklaces. Is there anything better than skipping class for a matinee?"

She flashed a smile at me. "A matinee and popcorn."

"Doesn't get any better than that. But what kind of popcorn?" I wasn't ready to let go of the moment. "Regular? Buttered or kettle corn?"

She rolled her eyes and parked her hands on her hips. "Is that some kind of trick question?"

I arched an eyebrow. She was playful. *Kill me now.* My kryptonite was a woman who liked to banter. "Maybe it is."

"Obviously, the answer is kettle corn."

We were *only* discussing popcorn. I knew that. Still, I felt like Hugh Grant in *Love Actually* when he meets the woman he falls for on his first day of work and knows, just knows, he's a goner.

"Good point." But I could have done her one better. What I could have said, but didn't, was *A matinee, popcorn, and a girl exactly like you.*

4

KAT

Present Day

He stood framed by Washington Square Park, the late afternoon clouds behind him.

"Fancy meeting you here," he said once I was within speaking distance.

What part of me bolting out of the classroom was hard to interpret? The anger that had uncoiled as I talked to my mom tightened back up again. Because he'd waited for me. Because he could be so easy and friendly in his manner, or else fake it really well. Because he seemed impervious to my ice-gaze, while with one look he could set off fifty different emotions in me like a long row of firecrackers.

"Who would have thought?" I replied, keeping my tone cool, at least. I reached for the movie camera charm and touched it once, as if it brought me power and strength. Nearby, a mime walked an imaginary dog and a grown woman in a Glinda dress created giant bubbles with a wand, to the delight of the toddlers chasing them.

"So, I was thinking," he said, in a here-goes-nothing voice that hinted he may not be as impervious as I thought, "I want this mentorship to go well and be useful for you. So, what if, for the sake of the class, we start over? Just wipe the slate clean and go on like we just met today."

"And what?" I asked, stunned that he thought I could flip the past hurt off with a switch. "Just reset the past like a video game?"

He raised an eyebrow. I didn't want to let on that I had this riot of feelings inside, but I couldn't seem to help it around him.

Changing his tone slightly, he tipped his head toward an open bench. "Want to chat for a bit?"

No. You broke my heart. I don't want to be near you in any way, shape, or form.

But if I couldn't switch mentors tomorrow, I'd have to work with him—be civil, at least. For now, a clean slate was a good approach. I could pretend he'd meant as little to me as I apparently had to him. After all, I'd been over him for a long time. Seeing him again had simply stirred old memories, like dust in an unused room.

So, playing along, I extended a hand and an all-business smile. "Nice to meet you. I'm Kat Harper. I'm an aspiring jewelry designer."

He shook my hand. "Bryan Leighton. A pleasure to meet you too. I run Made Here. We make things like this," he said, and fingered the onyx cuff links on his sleeves.

We walked to the bench, and I sat on the far end, hoping he'd take the hint. But he took the middle, ignoring all the empty space on his other side. With him this close, the memories closed in—how we couldn't keep our hands off each other that summer, how he was always touching my back, my legs, my waist.

I pictured profit and loss statements instead of the planes of his flat stomach, his firm chest, his sculpted arms.

He leaned an arm against the back of the bench, glancing down at my necklace. "Tell me about your jewelry designs, Kat."

If anyone else had asked, I'd say I always loved dressing up as a kid and rooting through my mom's jewelry box to find bangles and necklaces and rings. But they hardly fit, so I began making my own jewelry, first just stringing together beads and baubles from a kit and little charms on wire. In junior high, I sold some of my necklaces at local craft fairs, then moved on to heart pendants in high school. I was eighteen when I had the idea of making a charm necklace—something unique with special meaning to the wearer. A charm that celebrated the mistakes we made as we moved past them.

For Bryan, though, I kept it to the point. "They're charms that mean something to the wearer."

"My Favorite Mistakes," he said.

"That's it," I said, surprised he knew the name of my line.

He gave me a sheepish grin. "I like to stay on top of things. Know who's up-and-coming." I reminded myself not to read anything into it. He was a savvy businessman, of course he would pay attention to future trends, which I definitely hoped My Favorite Mistakes would be. He lifted his hand toward my neck, indicating my necklace. "May I?"

"Do you want me to take it off?" I asked, then inwardly winced at the accidental double entendre. Maybe he hadn't noticed.

"I like it on." Running a finger against a miniature skyscraper charm, he grazed my skin and a spark shot through me.

Oh, he'd noticed. I looked away so he wouldn't read my feelings in my eyes, and stared at the sky instead. The clouds had become grayer, with a heaviness to them that spelled rain soon.

"What's this one?" he asked about the skyscraper.

"A friend of mine in college had a lead on a supercheap sublease on the Upper East Side that I almost moved into before I started the MBA program. I didn't get the apartment, and I was devastated at the time."

"So you made a charm?"

I nodded. "It all worked out for the best. Because now I have a great roommate and an amazing place in Chelsea." I'd met Jill when I went to an odd little musical theater showcase in Hell's Kitchen and hung out with the cast afterward. She'd been the lead, but more to the point, she'd just nabbed a rent-controlled apartment in Chelsea, handed down to her by her aunt. She needed a roommate; my sublease prospect had fallen through. Result—we lived in one cheap, cool flat in Manhattan and Jill was now my best friend, even if she'd been practicing her latest audition piece in the living room over and over until I heard it in my sleep. Luckily, she was really talented.

"Chelsea is great. Very eclectic. Perfect for you," he said.

I tensed and stared at him sharply. "How would you know?"

"Know what?"

"What's perfect for me—how would you know?" I'd kept it civil and professional until now, but he'd broken the agreement that allowed me to do that. "We just met each other, remember? Your idea."

"Call it a hunch, then." Seeing how I'd dug in, he faltered a bit, abandoning a smile for a shrug. "It just seems very you. Chelsea, that is."

I tapped my chest with a finger. "But you *don't* know me anymore. I might as well be someone you just met, because you don't know a thing about me."

He nodded once, taking my rebuke on the chin. "I didn't mean anything by it. I'm sorry."

"For what? What are you sorry for, Bryan?"

"For . . ." he started, but then the Glinda-clad woman ran past us with a giant bubble trailing behind her and a band of children in pursuit.

I took a quick breath, reminding myself that

raking over the past would not help me let go of all these warring emotions.

"Chelsea is great," I said brusquely, and took the reins of the conversation, pointing to another charm, a silver book with the pages open. "I was an English major when I started college. But at the end of my freshman year, when a shop owner started carrying my necklaces, I switched to business. My almost-major is another favorite mistake." That was the back-story on the website for My Favorite Mistakes—still true and still personal, but less painful than the original inspiration.

He nodded. "I like that. Very smart decision, and a good way to acknowledge the road not taken. And this one?" He fingered the movie camera charm, his hand resting on the space just above my breasts.

My chest rose and fell, and I tried to steady my breathing and deliver an offhand answer. "Oh, that one. I just made that to remind myself not to spend too much time watching movies."

Because movies had been our thing. Our first kiss had been in a movie theater.

He was still touching the camera charm, but he was looking straight at me, as if he could read the lie.

I shifted the focus away from me and asked, as if I were a curious interviewer, "And you? What about your business, Mr. Leighton?"

He let the charm drop, and the metal was warm from his touch. Holding out his arm, he gave me a better look at one of the cuff links he'd shown me earlier. "These bad boys are our signature item." He seemed to be offering it for closer examination, but I resisted. "We make them at a factory near Philly, along with tie clips and money holders. But the cuff links took off like crazy a few years ago, when that book series came out with these on the cover, and they've continued to sell well to women buying them as gifts."

Of course they did. I banished thoughts of unbuttoning the black onyx, of taking off his shirt and watching the fabric fall away to reveal his smooth chest, his firm stomach, his trim arms. I focused instead on remembering whether I'd dropped an umbrella into my purse that morning, because the sky was about to split open.

"Right. Perfect gift." I stood up and brushed my hand over my skirt, then gestured to the clouds. "I better go."

He rose too. "You going back to Chelsea?"

"Yes."

"I'll give you a ride. I have my car."

"I'm fine," I assured him quickly. "I'll walk or take the subway."

"Kat. It's about to pour any second."

I patted my purse. "I have an umbrella in here."

"Wouldn't it just be easier not to fight for a cab, not to get soaked, and not have to take the subway?"

Before I could say no again, he had his phone out. He gave his driver our exact location just as the first drops hit my head. The rain picked up as we walked quickly to the curb, and moments later, Bryan held open the door of his town car for me. A raindrop fell in my eye; I blinked it away as I was climbing in and bonked my head on the top of the door.

A sharp pain radiated across my forehead. "Ouch!"

"You okay?" Bryan asked as he slid in next to me. The windows were tinted, but the partition was down. I could just make out the words to Jack White's cover of "Love is Blindness" on the radio. I almost asked the driver to change the channel because the lyrics turned my heart into knots of dark wanting.

I pressed my palm against my head where it smarted. "I don't know how that door got in the way of my head," I said, and Bryan laughed.

Then he gently replaced my hand with his. "Does it hurt?"

"A little," I whispered, letting down my guard for a moment. Brushing my dark brown bangs from my face, he held my gaze, chipping away at the walls I'd rebuilt in the last hour. I flashed back to the movie theater in Mystic, to our first kiss, when I had no defenses because I didn't need them.

"Do you need ice for it?" He removed his hand.

"Do you have ice?"

"Of course. Fully stocked."

"I think I'll be okay."

"Let me just check for a concussion," he said, and stared intently into my eyes like a serious doctor studying the signs. He was being playful, but I wanted to brush him away and insist I was fine, only I couldn't move. Inches away, I could feel the warmth from his body. I swallowed and glanced out the window, breaking the bizarre trance first.

"I take it I'm going to live?"

"I think you're in the clear." He pulled away, and I couldn't read him at all now. "What's your address?"

I gave it to him, and he told the driver, then he looked back at me again. His green eyes were darker, more intense. "It's really good to see you again, Kat."

Those conflicted feelings welled up again, and I grasped at numbers, at logic, at images of my parents' store, at the sound of my mom's voice. But they were all wisps in my hands.

The back of the car seemed to grow smaller and bigger at the same time. Everything faded away—the din of the music from the radio, the strangers on the street ducking under awnings and opening umbrellas as they sought cover. Bryan was all I saw, sitting next to me, looking in my eyes. I wished I could think of business, of my jewelry line, or even of mundane things like where I'd left the quarters for the next load of laundry, because that would all prove I was as impervious as I'd aimed to be. But my traitorous heart wouldn't let me think at all, only feel.

Somewhere, I found the strength to steer myself back on course. Keep it polite. Keep it light. "It's good to see you too." I gingerly rubbed my forehead. "Otherwise, who would have checked me for a concussion?"

He caught my change in tone and after a beat made his own pivot. "So, I was thinking it would be a good start to this mentor thing if I showed you the factory. Can you go with me on Friday?"

"Let me just check my schedule and get back to you."

Then I turned away and stared out the window as if the rain-soaked New York streets were endlessly fascinating, and mentally high-fived myself for playing it cool.

5

BRYAN

Five Years Ago

There's an unwritten rule that you don't date your friend's sister. Because if you break her heart, you're the ass who broke your buddy's sister's heart.

I tried to shake away the thought as we finished our pizza on the deck of Kat and Nate's parents' house that first night, chatting about the town of Mystic as Nate grabbed a refill of beverages.

"Tell me about Mystic. Are you a fan?" I asked, figuring the topic of her hometown might get my mind off how pretty she looked with the moonlight shimmering on her face.

She pointed to herself. "Number one fan. It's a small town, but if you like the smell of the sea and more nautical tchotchkes than you can handle, you'll love it here too."

"The scent of the sea is indeed excellent. And I am well known for my ability to handle knickknacks."

Her grin was playful, amused. "Then you and Mystic will get along just fine," she said with a happy sigh. "I do love this place. It's quiet at night, but full of character during the day."

"And charm. I bet it's got lots of charm," I said with a grin.

"Oodles of it. Bursting with charm," she said, in an over-the-top tone.

I spread my arms wide. "I'm sold."

"And of course, it's home, so it reminds me of family," she said, more contemplative now, then asked about my family.

I shared details of my parents in Los Angeles and my younger sister who lived there too.

"Is that home to you? LA?" she asked.

"Somewhat, but New York is in a way now, since I've been gone for a while."

"And do you love New York?"

"I do, but I'd love to travel as well," I said, and we chatted about that for a while. She was so easy to talk to, tossing questions at me like we'd known each other for years, listening intently as I answered. Crickets chirped and the warm night air surrounded us. Why did it have to be a perfect summer night, everything conspiring to make me fall for her?

Soon, Nate popped out again. "Sorry. I got caught up on a phone call. Hope you guys were able to pass the time."

And maybe I was a terrible friend too because I wished he were still on that call.

"We muddled our way through," I joked.

"It was horribly painful," Kat teased.

Nate rolled his eyes. "Did you still want that soda?" he asked his sister.

Kat yawned and passed on the Diet Coke. "I better go to sleep. Since I've got the Mystic Landing morning shift and all. You guys can stay out here and have your guy talk without me. No one needs the little sister around."

I was about to open my mouth to protest and say, *I do, I definitely do*, but she was already gone.

And I was already looking forward to working in the store with her the next day.

6

KAT

Present Day

I'd resisted internet stalking Bryan for the last few years, but I read the business news, and there were things that were impossible *not* to know. Like how his company was a generous supporter of the NYU business school and had endowed a new wing of the library last year. How he'd started Made Here four years ago, and it had grown quite nicely. Timing was everything, and he'd capitalized at the right moment with his product line. He knew, too, that the mood of the country had shifted and that people wanted American-made goods, so he retrofitted a former lug nut factory for manufacturing his line of men's accessories, and he, along with his business partner, had built Made Here into a thriving success.

That was just his professional life though. I hadn't tracked him on Facebook or Instagram or anywhere else in months. I knew he and Nate caught up with each other now and then, but I didn't ask for information. The less I knew, the better.

Besides, I'd had better things to do. I'd had a boyfriend in college, though he'd been more serious about me than I was about him, and that didn't turn out well. After I broke it off with Michael—because I didn't want to get married at twenty—he'd call and show up at my door at all hours of the night. When I was accepted into a study abroad program, I was almost as relieved as I was excited.

I studied in France for my senior year—I lived in the City of Lights, immersing myself in the language, the food, and most of all, the artisanal jewelry. My days were filled with cobblestoned streets and stone corridors of universities older than the United States, and my nights were rich with lamplight and a winding river and the occasional kiss with a young Frenchman. Once I returned to New York and started business school, there was no room in my brain to think of Bryan.

Now, I legitimately needed to do some research. I wanted to be prepared to petition my professor to switch mentors, and if I couldn't, I'd still need to know about who I'd be working with. For the first time in ages, I ran a search on him, as well as his company's name. The very first result was a surprise.

Made Here Business Partner Ousted by Board Following Affair.

The link was to an article in a New York newspaper from only a few months ago. I checked out the photo of Bryan's ex-business partner, a standard sort of average-looking guy. As I read the article, several lines stood out. "At the board's insistence, Kramer Wilco has stepped down as co-chief executive officer of Made Here, the high-flying manufacturing start-up that's been earning tidy profits in the last several quarters. Wilco admitted to being involved with an intern at the Made Here factory outside of Philadelphia. Wilco started Made Here with his business partner, Bryan Leighton, four years ago. Leighton did not return calls for comment, but a spokesperson said he will run the company solo now."

I slumped back in my chair. I'd had no idea this sort of scandal had struck his firm. Was Bryan the one who discovered the affair? How had he handled it? Was he cool and clinical? Or pissed off and fuming, like I would be? I googled Wilco next and clicked on an interview he'd done with a business news channel a year ago, after Made Here inked a new deal with a large retailer.

"What's the biggest challenge your company faces in the quarter ahead?" the reporter asked at the end of the piece.

"Honestly, now's not the time to talk about challenges. Now's the time to focus on our new partnership," Wilco said. It wouldn't have been a bad answer if he hadn't been curt and snappish. He wasn't the most affable guy, that was for sure. I imagined Bryan would have handled the interview much better, coming across personable as well as smart.

Then I shook my head. How Bryan would have

managed a hypothetical cable news interview was irrelevant, and his feelings didn't matter to me anymore. I read a few more articles on Made Here's business strategy, then researched the skate-wear gal so I was prepped for tomorrow. Then I shifted gears and tended to some online orders and email queries, checked out a few of my favorite European design blogs for anything new and exciting, and finally turned to my other classwork, working with laser focus.

It was nearly midnight when my roommate, Jill, with her dark-blonde hair and deep blue eyes, got home from what she described as an epic dress rehearsal in which the cast of *Les Mis* had kicked unholy musical ass. It was an off-Broadway revival with the twist of a modern setting and a rock arrangement of the score, and apparently, they had some eccentric personalities in the cast.

Her report had me laughing until I was breathless, and when she was done and I'd recovered, I shared my own news. "You will never believe what happened today."

"Tell me."

I told her every single detail of my afternoon. "Anyway, there's no way I can learn with the distraction of our past relationship. I'm marching into my professor's office and requesting a new mentor tomorrow."

Jill pressed her lips together like she really wanted to say something but was waiting for me to ask.

"What?" I sighed, folding my arms. "You're dying to tell me, so you might as well."

Then came a shrug and a knowing look. "It sounds like you're as distracted by him today as you are by your past with him. Maybe your feelings aren't so ancient history after all."

"Yes, they are," I said through tight lips. "Dead and buried like King Tut."

"Yeah, keep telling yourself that, kitty cat."

* * *

The next morning Jill woke me up bright and early by throwing a sports bra on my face. "Rise and burn, sunshine. Rise and burn."

I rolled over in bed and shielded my eyes. "Go away."

That made Jill jump onto my bed and bounce until I opened my eyes.

"How is it you can rehearse till midnight and have the energy to go for a run at seven in the morning?"

"I'm a vampire. I don't need sleep. I survive off the nectar of my Broadway ambitions. And let's not forget I was actually up past midnight listening to you tell me all about Mr. Hottie McCuff Links."

I swatted Jill with a pillow then sat up in bed.

Jill clapped. "I win. Let's go run."

She was already in her leggings, sports bra, and a tight T-shirt, her long blonde hair looped in a hair tie. It would be less painful to give in and exercise with her than to resist. Which was saying something.

"Fine." I brushed my teeth, yanked my hair into a ponytail, and pulled on workout clothes. We headed out and broke into a run on Twenty-Second Street, heading for the West Side bike path. The sun was rising, and it promised a warm, clear September day.

Jill ran with her arms tucked by her body, feet hitting the ground in a perfect runner's stride. She did cross-country in high school, when she wasn't being a theater geek. Now she does marathons. My sports specialty was walking. The one morning a week I ran with her, I spent twenty-five of the thirty minutes wondering when the torture would be over.

"What's your plan?" Jill asked, not even breathless. "How are you going to resist him during your mentorship?"

"I'm asking for a transfer. But even if I can't get one, resisting him isn't the problem. It's how to work with Mr. Clean Slate I-want-to-forget-I-dumped-you-but-also-make-sure-you-don't-have-to-walk-home-in-the-rain."

"Nice," she said, and I thought she was being sarcastic. But she gave me a sideways glance when I didn't respond. "No, really. That is sort of nice."

"That describes him perfectly. He was sort of nice when he dumped me."

"I know he broke it off, but I always suspected there was more to it. Like he got scared or something. And I bet he still carries a torch."

I rolled my eyes. "Bet he does not."

"I have a feeling," she said.

"Based on what? Your wild imagination?"

"Well, he did want to check you for a concussion," she joked as she slowed her pace. Delighted, I dropped into a more comfortable jog.

"Oh, sure. Clearly he's carrying a torch and not making light of my clumsiness."

"See? That's my point. He was smoothing over the moment *and* grabbing an excuse to get close to you."

"It was nothing. Because there is *nothing* going on between us."

"Right now there's not. You might be above internet stalking, but I'm not. You know he's single, right?"

I groaned. Why was she tempting me? "He's twenty-eight. I'm not surprised he's not married yet."

"No, I mean he's really single. Broke up for real with someone he'd been dating on and off for a few years," she said.

I had to stay strong. "If it was on and off, it'll probably be on again. And on the same subject . . ." I slowed down and made a megaphone with my hands. "He dumped me. Don't you remember why I started My Favorite Mistakes?"

"People change. Maybe seeing you made him realize the error of his ways." She gave a hopeful, encouraging smile, and I realized why she was taking this position. She was, in some ways, a hopeless romantic, wanting to believe anything was possible. She was an actress, was always trying to get in touch with emotions, and this was a helluva one to tap into.

But it wasn't going to be tapped.

"Look, I can't mess up this mentorship," I said

between heavy breaths from running. "Call me a freak, but I actually like my parents and want to help them. That means I'm all work and no play until the end of the fall semester."

"I'll believe that when I see it," she said playfully. "And I like your parents too."

"Good. That's why I can't go there."

She nodded sagely. "I get it. You're doing the right thing." Then the grin reemerged. "I still say I'm right about him wanting to play doctor though."

"You are evil."

"I know."

I shook my head, but I was smiling at her persistence. This was all hypothetical anyway. The rules were clear and strict—no messing around between mentor and student. I had too much at stake to risk pushing the boundaries, not the least of which was my own bruised heart.

7

KAT

Present Day

I knocked on Professor Oliver's door, but it was wide open. He was that kind of teacher. The door was never closed.

"Come in, Ms. Harper." He gestured to the chair near his desk. "I'm delighted about the assignments this semester, and I hope you are too."

I drew a deep, fueling breath, prepared to make my argument. "That's why I'm here, actually. While I have the utmost admiration for Mr. Leighton and all that he's achieved as a chief executive at his company, I'd very much prefer a mentor in the retail sector," I said, calm and confident, chin up. "I had really hoped to be matched with Lacey Haybourne, who founded the skateboard line, since we're both essentially in the fashion industry."

Professor Oliver raised his eyebrows and put

down his pen as if ready to listen, and I added the details of my reasoning and research. While I did, he nodded thoughtfully, as if considering my request, and for the first time since Bryan had walked into the classroom yesterday, I felt like I could exhale. That I wasn't going to spend the next three months playing emotional ping-pong.

My relief didn't last long.

"Those are good points," said Professor Oliver. "But the assignments are set."

"Why is that?"

His eyes turned intense, and he leaned forward, shifting from the usual jovial man to what he was—a tenured and respected professor. "Because I have reasons for my choices."

I gulped. This was a different side to him. I'd never heard him speak this sharply, this forcefully before.

He picked up his pen again—a fountain pen that reminded me of one I'd seen at the upscale Elizabeth's department store recently. He twirled it between his thumb and forefinger. "Let me shed some light on why I made the match. For My Favorite Mistakes to grow and become a powerful jewelry brand, you'll need to learn about scale. About production. About manufacturing. That's the field Mr. Leighton is in. And what I think your business needs most is that sort of symbiosis. Yours is smaller, his is multinational, but your businesses have shared attributes. And you will learn plenty from a company that has weathered storms and come out ahead."

"I understand, sir." I'd hoped to sway him with

logic and leave my personal life out of it. But still, Bryan and I had been involved. Surely a prior romantic relationship would be a good reason for a switch. "The thing is—"

But he cut me off.

"Ms. Harper," Professor Oliver said, gently but firmly closing the door on any more discussion. "Bryan Leighton will be your mentor, and it will be great for you. Thank you for your understanding."

Briefly, I weighed making one last push. But I wanted my private life, past and present, to remain private. I didn't want my professor, who apparently had a much tougher edge than I'd realized, to know about my romances. And maybe I needed to be more like him—to have a tougher edge so I could weather the storms.

Time to woman all the way up. To lean on the tough edge I had too.

"Thank you for your time," I said, rising from the chair and turning to go, deciding to take this as a challenge. And if the professor thought I would benefit that much, maybe it was worth the frustration of spending three months with someone I'd spent five years trying to forget.

"Oh, one more thing," he called before I reached the door.

I looked back, and he handed me a business card with a phone number. "My wife wants to give one of your necklaces to a friend. They're going to be huge, your jewelry. Can you give her a call?"

"Of course. Thank you, sir."

On the way out, I called Professor Oliver's wife, who did seem excited to hear from me. It seemed she didn't just want my necklace for a friend. She had much bigger plans and wanted to discuss them over lunch, so we agreed to meet later in the week. After I hung up, I used my phone to google her so I could go in prepared. But when I entered her full name—Claire Oliver—I found nothing to connect her to the retail jewelry business.

I'd have to wing it.

Then, I bit the bullet and emailed Bryan to let him know that Friday would work for a visit to his factory. When that was done, I stuffed my phone, with its Eiffel Tower case, underneath my e-reader, my wallet, and some tissues at the bottom of my purse, hoping out of sight, out of mind would rule the rest of my day.

Not that I was waiting for his reply. Not that I wanted to see him again. Not at all.

I'd picked out the perfect outfit to meet Professor Oliver's wife.

I zipped up my A-line skirt, slid into a pair of black pumps, and adjusted my purple scoop-neck top one more time. I'd snagged the shirt from a shop in Brooklyn that always had amazing deals on clothes so I could look sharp at the occasional business meeting without blowing my budget. My dark hair was blown straight, and I had just the right amount of makeup on, just lipstick and some mascara. I grabbed my electric-blue purse, a cute retro number, because it was large enough to hold necklace samples in different styles, lengths, and colors, as well as an assortment of charms.

I left the apartment and caught the subway to my meeting on the Upper East Side, checking my email on the way.

When Bryan's name appeared in my email, my skin tingled.

That was inconvenient.

And utterly annoying.

Control. In an exercise of self-control, I triple- and quadruple-checked the charms in the inside pocket of my purse, I appraised my lipstick in the train window, and I peered at the time on my watch. Then, as if I'd proven something to the judge and jury of me, I took a breath and calmly tapped on the note.

Kat—I trust we're still on for tomorrow? I'll send my car to pick you up at 9 a.m. if that works for you. Are you one of those rare breeds who can manage the morning without caffeinated assistance? If not, please let me know your preferences these days—coffee, tea, or one of those fluffy drinks with lots of milk and made-up sounding names.

(If I were an emoji sort of guy, I'd insert one here to show I'm joking, but I'm not an aficionado of smiley faces and/or internet abbreviations.)

My best,

Bryan

. . .

I read the note several times, always stopping at the same spot—*these days*. Had he truly forgotten my tastes? He'd known before that I worshipped at the altar of fluffy drinks with frothy flavors. Maybe he was simply playing along with the whole "we just met" thing he tried the other day in Washington Square Park. Or maybe he'd forgotten because I'd never really mattered to him.

Fine, it was just a coffee preference we were talking about. But I had my pride, and I didn't want to confess I'd try any drink with an -ino ending.

I hit reply.

Bryan—The time is fine. I'll take my coffee with a splash of cream, please.
    Best,
    Kat

I reread my note. It didn't sound like me one bit. Normally, I'd try to say something fun, like *Frothy drinks need love too*. But he hadn't earned the right to banter again. Besides, if I didn't let him in, he couldn't hurt me.

The train pulled into my stop and I exited, walking quickly up the steps and into the sunshine of a late Manhattan morning. As I waited for the light at the crosswalk, I glanced at the screen and saw Bryan had already written back.

Kat—Funny, I seem to recall you were rather fond of caramel-itos and mocha-treat-os. Wondering what else I'll learn about how your tastes have changed in the last five years. Oh, wait—we're starting over, so this is all new information to me. Black coffee with a touch of cream it is, then.

(No emoticon inserted here intentionally, even though I would wink if you were here in person.)

My best,

Bryan

Damn him. He *did* remember how I liked my caffeine.

Damn him for trying too hard. He should be a jerk. Because I didn't want to feel the tiniest zing race through me when I read his words, because he did remember details of me. But it was time for my meeting. As I walked into a small restaurant with crisp white tablecloths, stainless steel vases holding lilies, and waiters wearing perfectly knotted ties, I extradited Bryan and his coffee winks from my brain.

* * *

Mrs. Claire Oliver ordered a Cobb salad with the dressing on the side. I followed her green example, opting for a Caesar with light dressing. She drank iced tea, and I did the same. She was a pretty woman, with dark-blonde hair cut in a straight and sharp bob, haunting brown eyes, and creamy white skin. She wore a sea-green blouse, designer jeans that probably cost more than my rent, and a pair of suede cutout Giuseppe Zanotti heels that were the height of haute couture. She was impeccably put together, like a Hollywood star appearing on a talk show, and she was younger than I expected. Professor Oliver had to be in his fifties, but I was betting his wife was no more than thirty-five.

"Mr. Oliver tells me you're one of his best students," Claire said as the waiter walked away.

"He's very kind to say that."

"I'm sure he wouldn't say it unless it were true. He thinks you're going to be a superstar in your field. I wouldn't be surprised, either, because I think your designs are top-notch," she said, and she wasn't the warmest woman, but there was something admiring in her tone.

"Thank you, Mrs. Oliver."

"You can call me Claire."

"Claire." It felt funny to call her by her first name. She was my professor's wife, she was older, and she was so perfectly high fashion that I felt as if I should be deferential.

"Kat, the reason I wanted to have lunch with you is I have a proposition for you. Your designs have such great promise, and I absolutely see a tremendous market for them. But what you're lacking is distribution. I'd like to show them around to a few buyers I know, get the pulse of the market, and see if we can't get you into more stores."

There wasn't a chance I'd say no to her or to anyone making such an offer. Still, I wanted to know who she was working for, or if she was a middleman for herself. "That would be amazing. May I ask which stores or which buyers?"

She waved aside the question. "Don't worry about that. My connections are good."

I wanted to know more, but if she was taking a chance on me, I'd have to take a chance on her. We discussed more of the specifics, the cut she'd receive of sales, her plans for showing my line around, and her vision for how women around the country would be giving and receiving these necklaces as gifts come holiday time. I mentally crossed my fingers because maybe, just maybe, this could help me help my parents.

"Now, you said I could see more of your designs."

I opened my purse and took out my latest necklaces, showcasing an array of charms.

She nodded and touched each one. "Some of your designs have a modern and sleek look. But others have a sort of European sensibility. Where do your inspirations come from?"

"Definitely from Paris. I lived there for a year."

"Ah, the most wonderful city in the world," she said to me in French.

"There is nothing better," I replied in the same language, and talked more about our favorite places in Paris. I told her I adored the shopping in the

Marais, and that my heart would always be in Mont-martre with its curvy, cobblestoned streets, but that the best deals were to be found at the open-air markets. "The jewelry there, the charms and trinkets, and the things you never thought could be charms, like tiny teacups or birds, are a total steal."

"You are a woman after my own heart. I, too, love shopping at the open-air markets, with their fruit and flower vendors and vintage jewelry sellers, as much as I love the Champs-Élysées."

We chatted just a little more, and then she excused herself for the ladies' room. While I waited for her to return, I noticed a sharply dressed man enter the restaurant and walk toward a woman with wavy auburn hair, already seated. She lifted her face to him. He leaned down and kissed her, a long slow hold.

I looked away, feeling wistful after talking about Paris. I'd once thought it must be the most romantic city in the world, a city of love stories. It still had the power to stir my heart, because I loved the city. But love stories were only that—stories.

8

BRYAN

Five Years Ago

I was slated for the afternoon shift at Mystic Landing along with Nate, but I was outside the shop waiting for Kat when she arrived that morning, ready to work. If my choices were to sit around all morning waiting for Nate to finally get up, or to spend the time with Kat, there was no contest.

Maybe I'd learn she was annoying, a pain in the ass, or silly, which would be great. Problem solved.

Or I'd find out that she was just as sweet and funny and smart as I'd seen so far, and I'd fall harder.

Problem quadrupled.

But the gamble didn't keep me away. As she came down the sidewalk toward me, I gestured to her drink. "Must have just missed you at the café. Coffee too?"

"Caramel macchiato. Only froufrou drinks for this

girl." She leaned in close—so close I could smell her shampoo, some kind of tropical rainforest scent that made me want to thread my fingers in her hair and see if it was as soft as it looked—and dropped her voice to a secretive whisper. "I even got an extra shot of caramel."

I pretended to be scandalized. "So decadent."

"And you?"

I tapped the lid on my cup. "Just coffee. I like my coffee the way—"

She scoffed and waved me silent. "Spare me whatever version of that sexist joke you're going for." Rolling her eyes, she deepened her voice and said, *"I like my coffee the way I like my women—hot, strong, with cream."*

My jaw dropped. I wouldn't say something so crass. All my crass thoughts were filtered and dropped into a secure folder where I saved them for another time. "I wasn't going to say that."

"Oh. Sorry. How do you like your coffee, then?" she asked as she unlocked the door to the store.

Maybe it was her earrings, shaped like the Eiffel Tower, or the opportunity was simply too perfect to pass up, but I leaned in a little and answered in a low whisper, "Black, the way they drink it in Paris."

She seemed to shiver before she pushed the shop door open. I didn't read anything into her reaction, but I enjoyed it.

"It's my dream to go there," she said as she put her purse under the counter. "I want to visit all the boutiques and shops and see all the gorgeous jewelry. I want to be inspired by the designs."

"There's not much that's as inspiring as Paris." I pictured being there with her, having coffee at a café, kissing her next to the Seine . . .

"Have you been to Paris?" she asked, sounding wistful.

"Only once, but I hope to go back. I'm pretty fluent from taking French in school, and the company where I'm going to work has offices there, so it could happen." I made myself useful by straightening the shelves as she unlocked the register and readied the store to open.

"Ooh, are they hiring? Then I can go to Paris too," she said. Her brown eyes sparkled, like we had another secret.

"I'll go ahead and book a flight. We'll sneak away."

She stopped what she was doing and looked at me, her eyes catching mine. Had I crossed the line? I *felt* like I knew her, but I realized we'd actually just met. I hadn't had time to learn all about her.

"Let's do it," she whispered, surprising me again. "Let's go to Paris. We won't tell a soul."

I grinned. "Wander around the city. No one will know where we are."

"Get lost in Montmartre on a cobblestoned, hilly street."

"Where someone is playing old jazzy music on a phonograph and it floats out the window." It was like a slow dance, with each step bringing us closer to admitting what was happening.

"And then we'd—"

But I didn't get to hear what we'd do next, because the jingle of the bell over the door cut short our trip to Paris, and the first customers strolled in.

Time to get to business. Kat and I worked well together, which didn't surprise me. There was an unmistakable vibe in the air, and everything between us clicked.

When Nate arrived for the afternoon shift, Kat gave him a rundown of the morning business and crowd. "That all sounds great. Mom and Dad will be happy. What are you guys going to do now?"

"I think I might go see a movie," Kat said. "I know, big shock."

He rolled his eyes. "Of course. Movie junkie here. Are you going to go to the movies too?" Nate asked me, and I knew he wasn't giving me permission to take out his sister, but I nodded. It wasn't as if I'd said, *Nate, I'm totally falling for Kat and I want to know if it's okay if we sit in a darkened theater for two hours*, but it was as close as I was going to get to some kind of tacit yes. Eventually, I'd say something, I told myself. Just not yet. There wasn't anything to tell him anyway. Once there was something to say, I'd say it. For now, we were two friends going to the movies. Nothing more.

At the local cinema, we perused the list of movies and both picked a Will Ferrell comedy, then she turned to me. "I'm going to be totally honest here. I kind of have a thing for silly humor. I know it probably doesn't go with the whole I-want-to-go-to-Paris-

and-be-inspired-by-the-designs, but sue me. I think Will Ferrell is a comedic genius."

Straight shot to my heart.

"Kat, I don't know how to tell you this," I said in a mock-serious tone. "So I guess I'm just going to be blunt. Will Ferrell *is* a comedic genius, and the fact that you have recognized this cosmic truth means the kettle corn is on me too."

Her lips curved up, and I was pretty sure she could get me to do anything with her smile.

"Lucky me," she said.

"No," I corrected, feeling bold as we were surrounded by the smell of fake butter and the snapping of kernels. "Lucky me."

When the lights went down in the theater, we shared the popcorn, and there were a few moments when my fingers brushed hers and vice versa. Those moments were enough to make me entirely forget the scenes unfolding on the screen, because all I was thinking about was how my blood was racing faster and my skin was heating up from a sliver of a touch.

By the time we left the cinema, the movie was swiss cheese to me.

My brain was occupied with thoughts of Kat, what she liked, how well we got along, how she laughed at my jokes, how she teased me right back, and how I was going to have to find ways to spend more time with her.

I'd become that guy falling hard for a girl.

That's who I was that week, counting down the hours each day until our shared morning shift ended and we went to the theater. It was our routine, our habit, right down to the popcorn and the seats in the second row from the back. We worked our way through the marquee, seeing a thriller the next day, then catching a sci-fi picture, and after that we saw a movie with talking animals in it, starring a chipmunk as the lead character.

Kat laughed the whole time, and so did I. The fact that this girl had such a wild sense of humor was another chink in my armor.

When the final credits rolled, she stroked her chin and spoke in a deeper voice, adopting the persona of a pretentious movie critic doing a review show. "You know, Bob, this has shades of that talking raccoon movie that audiences fell in love with years ago. Do you recall John the Chattering Raccoon? It had similar themes, wouldn't you say?"

I nodded as if she were intensely serious. "Absolutely, Sally. Though I do have to say I feel John brought a bit more pathos to the lead role than the chipmunk did in this picture. A touch more empathy, don't you think?"

She pretended to consider my question, staring thoughtfully at the ceiling then returning her focus to me. "He did, especially in the scene when he rooted around in the garbage can. Do you agree?"

Then she cracked up, a deep belly laugh where she placed her hands on her stomach, and I couldn't help but laugh too. It was too fun to be with her. "He went after that discarded sandwich with such gusto and vulnerability, the likes of which you rarely see on screen," I said, because I wanted another laugh, and I got one.

We returned to our normal voices as we stood up and made our way out of the theater. "You've pretty much seen every movie, haven't you?" I asked.

"I've seen a lot of movies."

"Why? I mean, besides the obvious. That movies are fun. But why are you such an intense fan?"

"Isn't that a good enough reason? Just for entertainment?"

"Totally. So that's the reason?"

"Sure," she said with a little shrug that seemed to suggest there was more to it.

"All right, Kat Harper. What's the story?" I asked as we walked down the street, the afternoon sun warming us. I wanted to know everything about her. I wanted to understand her. "Tell me where your love of movies comes from. I mean, where does it truly come from?"

She took a deep breath. "I do love movies for the pure entertainment value. But I also love them because they kind of represent family to me."

I was utterly intrigued. "In what way?"

"All these big events in my life were marked by movies," she said as we walked past a local art gallery where a guy had set up an easel outside and was painting a vast open sky. "When Nate was in eighth grade and won the election for class president," she began, and my gut twisted the slightest bit at the mention of her brother, but I pushed the feeling aside to listen to her story, "we all went to see the rerelease of *Raiders of the Lost Ark* because it was this great action-adventure, and I gripped the armrest when Harrison Ford raced against the boulder. The time I was picked to design the cover of the junior high yearbook, we went to see *Ocean's Eleven*. That's just how we celebrated things. I even remember when my grandmother died. We went to the memorial service. I was twelve, and I read a poem at the service, and then we decided that we should see *Elf*. Which probably sounds like a weird thing to do after a funeral," she said, lowering her voice a bit as if that was hard to say.

I reached out to touch her arm, resting my hand against it briefly before I pulled away. "No, it doesn't. Not at all."

"It was really the perfect movie to see because I think we all just needed to not be sad every second, you know?"

"It actually makes perfect sense," I said, and she stopped walking and looked me in the eyes. This time there was no flirting, no wink and a nod. Just a truly earnest and caring look in her deep brown eyes, as if she was grateful that I understood her.

"But I guess it all started with my mom. She's a huge romantic comedy fan, so she started showing me all the great ones. *Sleepless in Seattle. Love Actually. Notting Hill. You've Got Mail*," she said, and we resumed our pace. I wasn't even sure where we were headed— to her house, to the beach, down the street. But I didn't care. I was with her, and I didn't want the afternoon to end.

I didn't want any of our afternoons to end.

9
KAT

Present Day

A sleek black car with tinted windows waited outside my building at nine on the dot the next morning. Then Bryan stepped out of the car, wearing dark jeans, a white button-down shirt, and a tie with cartoonish giraffes on it.

"Oh!"

He ran a hand down his tie. "Did the giraffes surprise you?"

"No. I just thought you were sending a car. I didn't realize you'd be in it."

"Since we're headed to the same place, I figured I could bum a ride. That okay?" he asked playfully.

"Of course. That's only sensible," I answered with humor I couldn't help.

He held the door open, and I slid into the car then smoothed out the soft folds of my green skirt as the driver turned on the engine and pulled away from the curb.

Bryan gestured to the drink holder. "As promised."

There were three drinks there, and I glanced at him curiously. "Someone joining us?"

"No. I brought you the coffee with a dollop of cream. I also brought a caramel macchiato." He flashed a flirty smile. "In case you were just pretending you liked drip coffee."

"Why would I pretend about something so trivial?" He'd seen through me, and I didn't want him to see that I liked it, so I kept my tone serious.

He held up a finger. "One, anyone who thinks coffee is trivial has never had a truly great cup of coffee. And two, I wanted to see if I could remember —" He broke off and corrected himself. "I mean, I wanted to see if I could guess what kind of coffee drink you actually liked."

I looked from the coffee to the macchiato to Bryan. I let my hand hover over the first drink, then the second, as if it were a shell game. "Hmm. Did he guess right? I wonder, wonder, wonder."

He raised his eyebrows expectantly. I reached for the coffee and took a drink. It tasted like bitter sludge. I wanted to spit it out. Instead, I took a long swallow and fixed on a fake smile. "Mmm. There is nothing like a cup of joe to get the day going."

"Damn." He shook his head. "I really thought you were still a macchiato girl. I even got an extra shot of caramel in it too."

I stubbornly took another drink, the harsh taste a

reminder not to give in, even if he'd remembered the extra caramel.

We'd only been driving for five minutes when the car slowed to a stop and the driver came around to open the door. I gave Bryan a quizzical look. "I thought we were going to Philly?"

"We are. By train," he said, getting out first and then holding out his hand.

I waved away his offer, and we walked together into the station, took the escalator to the tracks, and went into the first-class car. It was quiet and air-conditioned, with dove-gray leather-backed seats.

"Would you like the window?"

I nodded then sat down, wishing I didn't find manners such a turn-on. He sat next to me, his leg brushing against mine. I should have shifted a few inches away, but we stayed like that, legs touching, as the train pulled out of Manhattan and picked up speed.

He answered emails on his phone, and I read some chapters in a business book that had been assigned in one of my classes. The silence wasn't awkward, but I didn't know if it was a good use of mentor time.

As we sped through the suburbs on the way to his factory, I thought about what I'd ask anyone else if they were my mentor—if I'd gotten switched to the skate-wear founder, for instance. I'd want her to describe how she started her business. Since I'd decided to act with Bryan like I would any other mentor, I closed my book and did that.

"So, I've read the official story of how you started Made Here, but I'd love to hear it from you."

He looked up from his phone, and I felt an electricity, a tightly coiled line between the two of us. He could always make me feel as if he were touching me, even if we were inches apart. Maybe it was because he wasn't afraid to look me in the eyes or hold my gaze. The effect was heady, especially when it took me by surprise.

"Paris inspired me, actually."

It was as if someone knocked me out of time. There was a day that summer when we talked about Paris while we worked in Mystic Landing. He had to be thinking about it too.

"You were in Paris?"

He nodded, still looking me in the eye. "Right out of graduate school, I was hired to work in New York, but the company sent me to their Paris branch for a year instead."

"A year?"

He nodded. "Yes. I transferred there right after . . ." He trailed off, and I filled in the blank. *Right after he broke up with me.*

"It's okay. You can say it. Right after you broke up with me."

He sighed deeply. "Yes. Then."

I held out my hands. "See? You said it and we both survived. And now we go back to the whole 'we just met' routine. Good?"

He nodded.

Fortunately, talking about Paris was easy for me. "Where did you live?"

"In the Latin Quarter. Across the river from Notre Dame."

"Me too." I pictured the flat I'd shared with a trendy young French couple—the narrow staircase that wound up four flights, the cramped kitchen and even smaller bathroom. But from the window in the second bedroom, I had a view of the river and Notre-Dame, and beyond that I could see Sacré-Cœur. A torch singer living across the street used to fling her windows open in the evenings, and while she cooked, she'd sing in a voice like whiskey and honey about love gone awry. "So you went to Paris for work. But this was before Made Here?"

"Yes. The firm did a lot of business with small suppliers who made handcrafted special goods. High-quality watches, leather bags, wallets, and such. And I was able to observe some of the processes, the handiwork, the craftsmanship. It got me thinking I could do the same back in the States, but I had to capitalize on something that was on the cusp of being popular and wouldn't just be a trend. That's when the cuff link idea came to me. When I returned from Paris, I connected with Wilco," he said, referring to his former business partner. "He was the money guy. I was the idea guy. He raised the capital, and I started building the business. And voilà. Four years later, here we are."

I noted that he didn't say anything bad about Wilco, when it would be easy to disparage the man, given the trouble he'd caused for Made Here. "Voilà indeed. I take it you're fluent?"

"*Oui.*"

"*Moi aussi.*"

He raised an eyebrow and said in French, "Then I can flirt with you in French and it'll be like a secret language just between us."

Flirt. Secret. Us. What was he doing using words like that? Playing with my emotions? "A secret between us and the millions of other people who speak French."

I turned to look out the window. We were passing through a beautiful town in Pennsylvania, rushing by farmhouses and stately white homes with impeccably trimmed green lawns and shrubs.

He peered out the window too, and I was keenly aware of his body so close to mine. For a moment, I imagined how this could play out. The train would take a curve. I'd bump into him. We'd share a moment.

A part of me desperately wanted him to touch me. To run a hand down my arm, to brush a strand of hair from my cheek. But I knew better.

Because I'd thought I was over him, but I was wrong. I had been forcing him into an out-of-the-way corner of my mind for five years. Now, with him inches away, I knew all I'd done was white-knuckle it through, faking my way through every other relationship when all I was really doing was resisting him, even while he was gone.

He pulled his gaze away from the window. "The towns are so pretty, Kat. Don't you think?"

"Yes," I managed to say without melting into his arms.

"And sometimes I think they're even prettier five years later."

Was that some sort of veiled compliment?

Or maybe an olive branch?

I didn't know, so I answered truthfully. "There's no denying the towns are lovely."

Soon, the train pulled into Union Station in Philly. We both rose before it came completely to a stop, and when it did, momentum tipped me against him while he braced himself on the seatback. He caught me before I could fall the other way, and when I looked up, his eyes were darker than usual, full of unsaid things.

Here was our moment. If this were a romantic comedy, we'd stammer and blush and set out for a montage of sightseeing and holding hands, snapping cell phone pictures and trying on hats, while posing with exaggerated pouts.

Instead, I straightened my hair and grabbed my purse, murmuring, "Thanks."

"Don't mention it," he said, and gestured me down the aisle ahead of him.

People in real life had to be more sensible. Real hearts didn't break seventy-five minutes in and heal by the ninety-minute mark.

10

BRYAN

Five Years Ago

"Kiss her! Kiss her now!"

I swear Kat murmured that under her breath. Stifling a grin, I glanced over and saw her biting her thumb like it was all that kept her from shouting at the screen.

We were at the movies again. It was our thing.

After a missed email, and a missed text, and a missed phone call, the hero and heroine were still on unsure footing. Kat seemed ready to walk up to the screen, grab the backs of their heads, and press their lips together.

Hell, maybe I was too.

The hero pushed the button on the elevator, rode up to her floor, marched down the hall, and at her door, he took that deep breath and knocked hard. When she opened the door, her eyes lit up with hope and happiness. He'd come to tell her how he felt.

"I'm so crazy for you, and if I don't kiss you now, I'm going to regret it for the rest of my life," he announced.

"I don't believe in regret. I believe in kisses," she said, and the moment their lips touched, Kat stole a glance at me, only to find I was stealing a glance at her.

"Hi," I whispered.

"Hey, you," she answered, her eyes locked with mine.

There seemed to be an invitation in that look, but I knew, too, how important words were. When I reached a hand toward her, I went slowly, my eyes on her the whole time. At last I whispered, "Is this okay?"

"More than okay," she said softly.

I ran my fingers through her soft hair, then my mouth met hers, and we kissed until the credits rolled, slow, sweet, summer afternoon kisses.

Her lips were delicious, her smell intoxicating, her kisses were like a drug. The movie had taken us to another world, where the boy gets the girl and the girl gets the boy, and her kisses made me never want to come back.

This was the kind of kiss that could go on and on, like a slow and sexy love song that thrummed through me from the inside out.

When I broke the kiss, I leaned my forehead against hers, wanting to be closer to her. "Kat, I've wanted to do that since I first met you in the driveway the other day."

"You have?"

"Yes. You were so pretty, and then you were everything else."

She grinned. "I thought you were pretty hot when I met you too."

I wiggled my eyebrows. "You thought I was hot?"

"I'm sitting here in the movie theater making out with you. How is it a surprise that I thought—think—you're hot?"

"What can I say? I like hearing it from a beautiful woman," I said. She blushed, and I ran my thumb over her cheek. "It's adorable that you're blushing."

"Stop," she said playfully, and I silenced her protest with a quick kiss. This one didn't last more than five seconds, but it was the promise of so much more. More kisses, more moments, more than this one.

When it ended, she said, "I think you're everything else too."

I let myself be thrilled for a moment, then that thought brought up a troubling fact. "Part of that everything else is that I'm your brother's best friend. Are you going to be okay with that?"

"But I'm not going to tell Nate," she said.

"Of course not," I said.

"He doesn't need to know. And this is between us."

I didn't think she could be any sexier, but somehow she was right now—how she owned this choice. How this was about her, not about my relationship with her brother.

Maybe I was starting to believe in love at first sight. Because it was happening to me.

11

KAT

Present Day

The factory was all noise and motion—whirring, humming, rattling. Bryan gave me the guided tour of the whole operation, stopping along the way to talk with his employees, from the managers who ran the facility to some of the men and women at the end of the line who worked like master jewelers with loupes, carefully and painstakingly putting the finishing touches on pair after pair of fine platinum and pewter and silver cuff links for the line called Sleek.

Made Here also created cuff links for their Scuff line, made from recycled materials including old watches and bike chains that had a deliberately worn and tarnished patina. The factory had once made lug nuts for hubcaps. With his expertise in engineering and his vision for unconventional problem-solving, Bryan had retrofitted the factory for Made Here's goods, and the result was a mixture of automation and craftsmanship.

"You know what I really want most for the recycled line?"

"What would that be?" I asked.

"The lover's bridge in Paris."

"The one the city remodeled a few years ago?"

He laughed. "No. Just the padlocks that were removed."

On one of the bridges spanning the Seine, lovers had written their names on locks, hooked them to the links, and tossed the keys into the river as a promise. It had become so popular with locals and tourists that every year the old locks had to be cut off to make room for new proclamations of the heart. But in recent years, the city had taken the locks down in sections because they were weighing down the bridge.

"I've been trying to work with the city of Paris for years to buy the used locks from them. But French bureaucracy is, well, French bureaucracy."

The idea sparked my imagination, and for the first time since seeing him in my classroom that day, I spoke from the heart. "That would be amazing though. What a perfect gift. A pair of cuff links made from padlocks on the lover's bridge."

"Right? Wouldn't it be? They just go to waste, but what if I could take those off their hands and turn them into something beautiful and meaningful?"

"Do you think it'll happen?"

"I've made some headway. But it's not a project I

can delegate. I'm the only one at the company who's fluent enough to converse with French bureaucrats."

"Well, if you need any help, you know where to find me. But you should know, I charge a fee for my translation services."

That earned a brief smile. "Let me show you more of what goes on here now." He pointed to the machines running with precision timing to move the parts along. "Automation lets us turn out product quickly and fulfill larger orders." We stopped next at a section of the factory floor where workers took their time turning the material into new shapes and sizes.

One of the guys who was assembling parts from used bike chains gave Bryan a quick nod.

"Hey, Joe," Bryan said.

"Hey, Boss Man," Joe said.

"How's the wife? Does Megan have her teaching degree yet?"

Joe nodded. "Just a few more months and she'll be able to start working in the school district."

"That's fantastic. Keep me posted."

So, Bryan knew his employees' wives' names, and what they did for a living. As we walked on, I thought about how if he were a jerk, it would be much easier to dislike him and keep him at a distance. But it was getting harder to pretend he was nothing to me.

We popped into a glassed-in area where a dozen people in white lab coats were doing the finishing work on the cuff links, tie clips, and money holders. "Looking good, guys. I'm psyched about the progress you've made this month. Make sure Delaney knows how you take your coffee or latte or whatnot. We'll do a pick-me-up order from Stella's later," he said, and I assumed Stella's must be the local coffee shop. "On me."

There were cheers behind us as we headed to Bryan's office on the second floor. His assistant, Delaney, cradled a phone receiver as she scribbled down elaborate notes. She was cute and perky and had a librarian sexiness to her, with black glasses and blonde hair fastened in a bun.

Bryan held the door and motioned me ahead into his office, which was functional but it didn't scream "executive." There was a large wooden desk, a gray couch, a navy-blue chair, and a few framed awards on the wall. I checked them out—they were from the Eco-Alliance. The train, the car, his entire recycled line . . . Bryan didn't just talk the talk.

Another chunk of my ice-wall came down.

He gestured me toward the chair in front of his desk, and for the next hour, we talked about the manufacturing process, his distribution strategy, and some supply chain challenges he'd been facing lately.

He was just going into detail about them when Delaney knocked on the door, popped her head in, and asked if it was time for the Stella's run.

"The usual for me," Bryan said. "Kat? You want something?"

"An iced tea would be great."

Bryan angled his head as if he was trying to figure me out. I knew he expected one thing from me, but I gave him another. That was intentional, though when it came to the coffee this morning, I may have been proving my point the hard way.

He turned his attention back to Delaney in the doorway. "I told the finishing crew that drinks were on me, so if you could see what they'd like as well. And don't forget yourself."

"Oh, I won't," she assured him as she left.

We got back to work, Bryan asking me about My Favorite Mistakes and how I envisioned growing the business. I had to confess that I didn't entirely know, but it was easier to admit after spending this time with him, seeing him not just as a savvy businessman but a conscientious employer.

Delaney returned shortly, carrying a cardboard drink holder with an iced tea and a coffee.

"Those papers you requested from the board concerning the Wilco termination should be in your email," she told Bryan, setting the drinks on the desk. "I've summarized their comments so you can be ready for your two p.m. call."

"Great. Thank you. I look forward to reading what they have to say." He didn't look eager at all, but Delaney didn't seem to take it personally. As she left, closing the door behind her, Bryan glanced at me, as if watching for a particular reaction. "She's very involved and eager to learn. She has a lot of responsibility."

He didn't have to explain why his admin assistant was reviewing paperwork. "I imagine keeping your act together is a huge responsibility," I said, straight-faced.

Laughing, he reached for the coffee she'd set on the desk. It was wedged in the carrier, so he slid the cardboard tray closer to him. "She makes me look good when I go before the board, it's true. And not just by making sure I'm adequately caff—"

He'd been paying more attention to talking than to wrestling the to-go cup from the holder. The cardboard was stubborn—until it wasn't. When it released, Bryan's tug turned into a jerk, the lid came off the cup, and coffee splashed all over his dress shirt.

We both froze for a startled second and then . . . I started to laugh. It started small and built into uncontrollable guffaws. It felt *so good*. I was always so worried about success and my parents, it felt like forever since I'd let loose, and I couldn't believe it was with Bryan.

On the other hand, I couldn't imagine feeling free to laugh with anyone but Bryan, and the wounded look he exaggerated didn't help.

"That's all the sympathy I get?" He shook his head sadly, placing the half-empty cup on the table. "The world is a cruel place."

"I'm sorry," I said between chuckles, wiping my eyes.

He flashed me a grin that was like the sun coming out from behind the clouds—manufactured clouds, but still—of his woebegone expression. "Liar."

I didn't deny it, but I did get control of myself. "It didn't burn you, did it?"

"No, I order it less hot. I like to be able to drink it right away." When he stood, the front of his white shirt looked like coffee-colored modern art. "But I was thinking ready to drink, not ready to wear."

A giggle threatened to pop out. "Don't get me started again."

He grinned like there was nothing he'd like better, but just walked to a small closet in the corner of the office and took out a new shirt. It didn't surprise me that he kept clothes here.

It did surprise me a little that he started unbuttoning the shirt he was wearing.

I cleared my throat and started to rise. "I'll just, uh . . ."

He froze with his fingers on the buttons. "I'm sorry. I didn't think—" He broke off like he had some choice words for himself, then to me said sheepishly, "Talking with you like this, I forgot you were a student. I didn't mean to make you uncomfortable."

"Oh, I'm not uncomfortable," I assured him in a rush. "Unless you're uncomfortable. Are you uncomfortable?" If I was flustered, it was because I'd felt the same way—like we were business associates, not mentor and mentee. He took my ideas seriously, and that was almost as hot as watching him reach for one of his cuff links and, when I sat back and pretended to be at ease, deftly remove it.

"No," he said, watching me as if he knew what I was thinking. "I'm not uncomfortable." He took off the other cuff link and laid them both on a nearby bookshelf, then he shrugged out of his shirt, stripping down to his undershirt.

"Your, um, T-shirt is stained too," I pointed out.

He glanced down with an exaggerated sigh. "That's never coming out."

"Maybe you'll get more for Christmas. Nate always loved when our parents gave him underwear for Christmas when he was little."

"When he was little? Your mom was still sending him new underwear in college. I don't know what she thought he was doing to go through it so fast."

"Better not to know," I said.

"Agreed." Bryan grabbed the hem of his T-shirt, but before he pulled it off, he looked at me as if for permission. I waved a careless "go ahead," but like anyone could have pried me from my seat. I could pretend it was curiosity, that I wanted to see how he'd changed in five years. But one thing I could tell hadn't altered a bit was my desire for him.

Maybe he was playing it cool too, but he pulled off his T-shirt and went about getting a clean one from the closet, leaving me free to drink him in. His chest was broad and firm, his arms strong, and his stomach as flat as the earth before Columbus proved otherwise. There was the slightest trace of hair running from his belly button to the waistband of his slacks.

I looked away. This wasn't going to work.

Not the mentorship—that was working fine.

But this pretending I was impervious to him. That he didn't stir up feelings as well as memories. That I didn't notice all the ways he showed me that, whatever had happened before, in this do-over he had feelings too.

"Hey," I heard him say softly. I focused on him,

startled to see he'd crossed the office and stood right in front of me wearing a clean shirt.

"Hey," I echoed, watching his fingers work the buttons through the holes.

"Where did you go?" he asked, and when I frowned in confusion, he went on to explain, "You were miles away for a moment there."

I recalled the first day in class and reached up to rub between my brows. "Was I frowning?"

"No." He reached out, slowly enough that I could have moved away if I'd wanted, and tucked a strand of hair behind my ear, his fingertips brushing my skin as he did.

I imagined leaning into his hand, purring like a cat. Imagined him tracing my bottom lip with his thumb as he still cupped my cheek, tilting my head up as he bent down and touched his mouth to mine . . .

I met his gaze, searching to see if he felt the same thing. And yes, all that and more. All I had to do was lean in just a little.

Or I could be sensible and lean back, smooth my skirt with my palms, and say, like my mother, *Right. Let's get to work.*

Before I knew for sure which I would do, Delaney's voice boomed through the buzzer. "Hi, Bryan. Just a reminder you have your call with the board in ten minutes to go over the final Wilco papers. The notes are in your email."

Bryan cursed under his breath. "Thanks, Delaney," he said in a perfectly professional voice. When she hung up, the longing had been stripped from his eyes.

He was a man ready to conduct business. "I have to do this."

I waited for him to acknowledge that we were in a moment. That he wanted to kiss me, that this timing sucked. But he was already, as he had put it, miles away.

Ouch.

Don't be ridiculous, Kat. What's a moment, really? What does that even mean?

He'd been thoughtful, and he'd implied he enjoyed talking to me. That was all.

Stepping back, he finished buttoning his shirt and retrieved his cuff links. He didn't say we'd get back to our discussion when he was done, didn't ask me to stick around, didn't ask me to dinner. He simply said, "I need to focus on this call."

But what I heard were echoes of "I have to go" and the silence of the disconnected call.

"Of course." I downshifted to a crisp and businesslike tone. I could go toe to toe with him in this department.

"But let's take the train back to New York. The four o'clock, okay?"

"Sure." I gathered my bag and my books. "I'll just be"—I waved in the general direction of the door—"not in here."

He settled into his desk chair, his eyes already on the computer screen and the email with the Wilco notes. He sighed heavily and dropped his forehead into his hand. "Fuck," he said in a low voice, and I suspected he wasn't going to have a very good phone call with the board.

I grabbed my iced tea, left his office, and said goodbye to Delaney. Then I called a cab as soon as I left the factory. There was a two-thirty train back to New York that had my name written all over it.

12

KAT

Present Day

The music drowned out my thoughts, and I wasn't complaining.

At a bar in SoHo, we celebrated opening night of the month-long run of the *Les Mis* off-Broadway revival Jill had been rehearsing so hard. The show itself was amazing—the producers had staged the story in modern-day France and added guitars and drums to the orchestra.

Somehow not exhausted from a great performance, she and her castmates had grabbed guitars and jumped on stage to jam out to "One Day More" performed as a power ballad. Jill could handle a guitar —she jammed hard on her Stratocaster and the amps howled out chords. Reeve and Caden, the two guys who played Marius and Enjolras, whipped the audience into a frenzy. Caden, with dark-blond hair, led the song. When he reached the chorus, he thrust the mic toward the crowd and they all joined in with gusto. Most of them were in the cast, and anyone who called themselves a musical theater fan knew the words. I was pretty sure the non-theater people had bailed.

My brother, Nate, was over at the bar refilling our drinks. I raised an arm and sang along, the whole lot of us jammed together in front of the tiny stage. Caden was a certified babe in an arty sort of way. He was tall and lanky, wore hipster jeans and a T-shirt with a vest. His hair was deliciously disheveled. Jill had mentioned him before, and that he was good-looking. She'd also said she had no interest in dating him because it was a bad idea to get involved with people you work with. Good advice indeed.

Caden was the total opposite of Bryan Leighton and his hot-and-cold, business-before-romance attitude. He had called me a few times after I took off from his factory that afternoon, but I didn't pick up. He'd emailed too, wanting to know where I was. If I was okay. If something was wrong.

My reply was simple: *I forgot I had an appointment in the city. The factory is amazing, and I am learning so much.*

His radio silence the rest of the evening just confirmed that I'd made the right choice to bail. He didn't seem to have a clue why I might be upset at being dismissed so abruptly—again. He hadn't thought of me until after his call, and clearly not since I'd reassured him I was fine.

Caden and Reeve belted out the final verse to the song, then mimed strumming a guitar solo alongside Jill as the song faded to its end. "Thank you so much for coming to the show and hanging out with us afterward. You are a kick-ass audience, and you rock my 'Red and Black' world," Caden said, and several women shrieked and held their arms out toward him.

As the singing actors put away their instruments, I found my brother at the bar. He handed me a vodka tonic. I'd probably only have a sip. I'd never been much of a drinker. "You sure you're old enough to drink?" he asked.

"Oh, haha. Two years on, and that joke never gets old."

He shook his head playfully. "You still seem like the baby sister to me."

"Well, duh. I always will be."

I was glad Nate took me up on the invite to come to opening night of Jill's show. We hadn't seen each other in weeks. He was on the road a lot, working in business development for a start-up, but he hoped to switch careers and move into the hospitality business. He'd just married the woman of his dreams, a talented sculptor named Joanna, and now he clinked my vodka tonic with his beer, and said, "To good music and my little sister."

If you looked closely, you could tell we were

brother and sister. We had the same cheekbones, high and sharp. But where I had brown eyes and even darker hair, Nate had scored light-brown hair and amber eyes.

"How are Mom and Dad? How did they seem when you were there?" I asked. Nate had visited them earlier in the week on his way to see a client in Boston.

"They're hanging in there. Dad's a little nervous about the loan coming due, I suspect, but Mom's Mom. All stoic and tough and 'we'll get through this.' She's trying out a few sales and mixing up the inventory a bit to see if that sparks some interest. And get this—she's doing one of those online daily-discount type of deals next week."

My mom had always been more of a traditional marketer, depending on foot traffic and tourist bureau promotions. That she was trying new things like online deals was perhaps a good sign. "I think I'm going to take the train out and see them tomorrow. I need to get away for the weekend."

Nate raised an eyebrow, and I realized I'd said more than I intended. "Why? Don't tell me there's some dude you're running away from?"

I fumbled with my glass and sloshed my drink on the bar.

"I guess I was right," Nate said knowingly, as he grabbed a napkin to clean up.

"That was just a really strong drink."

"Strong? Sure. I'm sure it was so strong it took till your third sip to spill it. Now, spill. But not your

drink. Who is he? And what did he do to you?" Nate
made a fist with one hand and smacked his other
palm. "Because I will seriously hurt him."

I laughed nervously. "It's nothing," I said, because
it was nothing. What happened with Bryan was truly
nothing. Besides, Nate and Bryan weren't best
buddies anymore, but they kept in touch, so I didn't
need Nate to know. "I swear. Just someone at business
school I liked isn't into me."

"Is he crazy?"

"Maybe." I was relieved when Jill came up and
bumped her hip against me. Caden was by her side,
and the traces of stage makeup gave him a sexy,
heavy-lidded look. Reeve must have taken off.

"Were we awesome or were we awesome?" Jill
asked.

"You were the freaking bomb." She was stunning as
Eponine, belting out a Pat Benatar-esque version of "On
My Own," and that encore of "One Day More" was just
as spectacular. I told her as much, then made introduc-
tions—Jill and Nate, and Nate and Caden. They ordered
drinks, and as the guys chatted, Jill pulled me aside.

The club had started blasting recorded music, and
we had to stand close to hear each other. No chance
of eavesdroppers, at least. "How did it go today? Did
anything happen?"

I pressed my teeth against my bottom lip and
shook my head.

Jill pointed at me. "That's your tell. When you do
that thing with your teeth. What really happened?"

"No, really. Nothing." At her continued stare, I gave in—she wasn't going to believe me otherwise. "But there was a moment when I wanted something to happen. Does that count?"

"Hell yes! Because you know the chemistry must be off the charts if it makes you all hot and bothered just thinking about being with him. I went out with a singer in a band—Stefan—and oh my God. One of those guys who all he does is look at you and"—Jill touched my arm with her finger and made a sizzling noise—"you are five thousand degrees of hot for them."

I returned the doubting stare she'd given me. "So, where is this Stefan now?" I asked, knowing the answer. "Are you dating him?"

Jill shook her head.

"See? That's my point. I don't want just the chemistry department. I want the whole package, and it seems clear I'm not going to get it with Bryan." I brought my voice back down from the heights of tension where it had climbed. "Which is all academic anyway, because I can't have chemistry or anything else with him while he's my mentor."

Jill sighed heavily. "Fine. Be that way." She tipped her forehead to Caden. "I know someone who might want to take your mind off Bryan."

"He is cute," I admitted.

She nudged me with an elbow. "He thinks you're a hottie too. Let's go chat."

When we returned to the boys, Jill struck up a

conversation with Nate, and Caden moved closer to me. "So, you liked the show?"

"It was great."

"What did you think about the modern feel of it?"

"It was the best. 'Master of the House' was like a Jay-Z rap, and when you sang 'Red and Black,' you sounded like the lead singer of Arcade Fire, and they're only my favorite band ever."

"Arcade Fire pretty much sets the standard for musical awesome. They're amazing."

"And so was your show. I was definitely into it."

"What else are you into, Kat?" he asked.

I wasn't sure if it was a prelude to a line, so I answered him directly. "Movies. I like movies. You?"

"I'd like to star in some movies," he said. "I have an audition next week for a Wes Anderson film."

"Wow. That would be incredible."

I'd dated an actor once and it hadn't worked out, but Caden had the self-confidence Michael lacked. As we talked about our shared love of all things Wes Anderson, I let my mind wander to his mouth, imagining what it would be like to kiss him. His lips were red and full, and he smelled of sweat and beer and the adrenaline of a fabulous opening night. I bet he tasted good, like charisma, like stage presence. And maybe I could enjoy it on some other night, but not this one. Tonight, no kiss could compare with the one I hadn't gotten.

When the night wound down, Caden and I parted ways, and I had to admit the truth, even if I couldn't do anything about it.

I was caught up in Bryan, despite trying to protect myself. He was the one I wanted. I'd told myself not to jump back into the fire, but that advice was useless when I'd never really left it. I'd never stopped wanting him.

If only Bryan wanted me in the same way. Body and heart.

13

KAT

Present Day

I spent the weekend working with my parents at their store, which took my mind off of Bryan. I prepped with my mom for her online deal and helped my dad sort through some overdue bills. I even slipped one from a vendor into my purse. I'd pay that bill myself, thanks to an order for ten necklaces that had been placed online over the weekend from a shop on the Upper West Side.

My parents took me to the train station on Sunday night, and walked me to the tracks. My mom still had a visible limp from the car accident and probably always would, but she kept up.

"I know why you came out this weekend, my Katerina." My mom was the only one I let use my full name.

"I came here to see you guys," I said, trying to dodge and dart.

She gave me a sharp, stern look, the kind only moms can give. "You're worried about us. But we're going to be fine. The store is going to be fine."

"Yes, you need to focus on finishing school, not checking up on us," my dad said.

"I took care of My Favorite Mistakes in the evenings, and I did homework when there weren't any customers," I said, then winced. I shouldn't have brought up the obvious. But then, maybe I should. The sagging store was the elephant in the room, and they were trying to deny it. I was struck by the realization of how very alike we were. The three of us trafficked in everything-is-fine-here attitudes, but inside we were trying to stiff-upper-lip-it through life's challenges.

"And that's what you should focus on, Kat." My dad pulled me in for a goodbye hug.

I hugged my mom next as my train pulled into the station. But before I boarded, I looked back at them, gathered up my courage, and said, "I know times are hard for you guys. I'm going to help. I promise. I have a plan."

Then I hopped on the train and waved. I didn't want to give them the space to tell me no.

* * *

The next few weeks raced by in a blur of studying for my Innovation and Design class and my management course. I took copious notes during school hours and did copious research for homework reports and projects. I snuck in some time to check trends on the latest European design blogs, but the rest of my hours went to tending to business—bringing custom orders to boutiques that carried my line and fulfilling online sales. I was wearing a tread on the sidewalk from my apartment to the nearest post office.

I stayed up late and woke up early, and I was exhausted, but I couldn't complain because My Favorite Mistakes was on track for a strong quarter, and I would be able to peel off a little bit to help my parents. It wasn't enough, but it was a start.

Meanwhile, there'd been no word from Claire Oliver, but I kept checking my email and phone, hoping for an update from my professor's wife.

And despite all that, work and school were still the easiest part of recent weeks.

The real challenge was avoiding one-on-one time with Bryan while there was so much to learn during my mentorship time with him.

The first time I went to his Midtown offices, I sat in on a meeting where the design team presented the newest additions to the holiday line for Bryan's approval. When the meeting was over, I slipped out of the conference room as quickly as I could, but he followed me down the hall, calling out, "Hey, Kat."

I stopped, wishing I'd had time to shore up my defenses. He'd been in his element in the meeting —decisive but open-minded as he listened to his team, the boss but still approachable. Not only was it attractive—because manners are so sexy—but it made me question my certainty that he would drop me, just like before, as soon as I was inconvenient.

Someone could be a good boss but a bad boyfriend though. I kept that thought in mind and turned around, trying to look cordial and not like I was making a run for the elevator. "Yes? Did you need something?"

He squinted slightly, like he was trying to see into my head. "I wanted to know what you think of the additions." This guy who'd just confidently signed off on a huge new manufacturing run wanted to hear my opinion.

That was the point of the class.

To learn. And to learn from him.

"They're great!" I started with, but that sounded so insincere, so I tried to save it with a double thumbs-up, which made it worse. Like politicians-kissing-babies worse.

Bryan hadn't missed the weirdness, still looking at me like a lab experiment. "Can you discuss them with me? I want to hear your detailed feedback."

Right. This was how mentorship worked. I was here to show him what I knew so he could coach me, not to give him cheesy thumbs-up or act like a yes-woman.

So, standing in the elevator lobby, I shared my thoughts. My detailed, analytical, business-focused thoughts. Speaking with authority outside of the classroom was different than taking a test, and I sounded so professional I surprised myself a little bit. I was suddenly really glad he'd stopped me.

"Terrific," he said, nodding. "Great insight. If you have time, I would love to—"

He motioned back toward his office, and it was impossible not to think about Philly, about how I'd lost sight of who and where we were. At that time, I'd wanted him to kiss me as much as I'd wanted to stay businesslike. I wasn't sure how to balance all those wants then, and I wasn't sure how to now either.

But since I had a class, I didn't have to make a decision.

"Another time?" I asked, backing toward the elevator. "I have an evening lecture in twenty minutes. I have to go."

"Of course. I look forward to it."

The scary thing was I did too.

* * *

The next week I ran into him at the water cooler, and he asked, "How was the lecture?"

"It was great!" I said. "We had a guest speaker, this venture capitalist who talked about calculating acceptable risk." The lecture had energized me, and I shared a few details with Bryan, who seemed to enjoy the topic too and weighed in with some of his own experience.

It felt productive and professional, but friendly— what I'd imagined a mentorship to be like. Especially when later that week he called out to me from the conference room as I was walking by and asked me to check copy for an ad slated to run in *GQ*.

"You're reviewing ad copy?" I asked, coming over to where he had a number of samples spread out on the table. A CEO's role in marketing was usually more at a budget and branding level. "Do you typically get involved with those details? Is that something you'd recommend for a business owner?"

"If you can fit it in. It's definitely wise to have your finger on the pulse of how the company is presented to the outside," he said. "Don't you agree?"

I nodded slowly, wanting to get the answer right. "It sounds wise to me." In my conversation with Professor Oliver in his office, he'd said my fledgling business would have lateral similarities with Bryan's company, but I was learning even more than I thought I would.

We stood shoulder to shoulder and studied the ads. I slid one front and center and gestured to it. "I like this one, but maybe just move the tagline over here. Otherwise, it distracts a bit from the image, and you want customers to focus on that."

"We do?"

I jerked my gaze to him, but he was smirking.

I rolled my eyes. "Fine. Cover up the product," I said, deadpan too. "I'm just the apprentice, what do I know?"

"Plenty," he said, and I smothered a satisfied smile.

We discussed a few more ads, then I checked the time. "This was fun, but I have to go."

He looked up from the table, surprised. "Now? Where are you off to this time?"

"Just to meet with Nicole. I was on my way there, actually . . ."

"When I held you up," he finished, nodding. "I appreciate you stopping to give your input."

"I had a little time."

"I'm glad you're finding her a good resource." He seemed about to say something else but changed his mind. "Have a good meeting."

I dashed off to see Nicole Blazer, a smart and stylish pint-sized redhead. She was one of Bryan's early business advisors on the design side, and also served on the company's board. She spoke with a Lauren Bacall huskiness that seemed at odds with her petite frame. My surprise must have been the usual reaction, because when we first met, she'd shaken my hand and said, "I don't smoke. Never have. Just blessed with this voice."

"Very *Key Largo*," I'd said with a grin. She'd laughed, and we'd gotten along well since then.

I stepped into her office, and she gestured to an array of tie clips and money holders on her desk. "Prototypes for a new line. Your job is to be a fresh pair of eyes and tell me what sucks and what doesn't suck."

She was refreshingly direct—no mixed messages with Nicole Blazer. I pointed to a gold money holder. "I have this theory that gold is becoming passé."

"Gold 'passé'? How's that frigging possible?"

"Well, not *gold* as in the only thing that actually

keeps its value. But gold jewelry. Rose gold is all the rage."

"Right. Of course."

"But it's too late to get ahead of that trend. So, what you need is the next thing after rose gold."

"What would that be?"

I flashed back to the Impressionist art I loved, the way the painters played with light and shadow to show different times of day. "What if it were possible to make a sort of sunset gold? Or morning-light gold? Rose gold is basically just a tinting. Maybe the same could be done with your tie clips and money holders. It would look as if the gold is reflecting the time of day."

She nodded appreciatively. "Damn, girl. I like that idea."

I'd also spent time with the operational team. I'd weighed in on some challenges they were facing with suppliers, suggesting strategies to spur along some of the more difficult ones. John Walker, head of operations, had even implemented some of my ideas. But a new wrinkle in the supply chain woes emerged later that week.

"Silversmith in Brooklyn said they're not going to be able to meet the timeline with bike chain parts," John said during a meeting. "We need to come up with a replacement within a week."

Bryan's features tightened, and he rubbed his hand over his chin. His green eyes were hard and intense. He didn't look at me once, and that was fine with me.

The meeting continued on like that for another

hour, and when it ended without a clear resolution from anyone, Bryan said he was going for a run. I took that as a cue to leave. Besides, I needed time and space away to try to research possible replacements for Silversmith. I stopped in the temporary office to grab my bag, and then headed for the elevator banks. I sucked in a breath when I saw Bryan there, wearing a gray T-shirt and running shorts. He pressed the down button.

"Hey." His jaw was still tight. The stress of the meeting and the supply complications was taking its toll.

"Going for a run?" I mentally slapped my forehead because he'd just said that he was. Also . . . running shorts. "Of course you are. Stupid question."

The running shorts were the reason I blurted out the first thing in my head. The shorts and those leanly muscled legs.

"It's not a stupid question," he said. "I could be headed for the gym."

I pointed to the strap on my own shoulder then to his broad and unencumbered ones. "Nope. No gym bag."

He paused to think. "Salsa dancing class?"

"In those shoes?" I asked.

We both lapsed into thought. Then I burst out with "Tai chi" at the same time he said, "Pilates."

Both ideas were ridiculous when I pictured them, and we exchanged a grin, gazes meeting for long enough that I could feel myself start to blush, and I cleared my throat as I glanced away.

Still, it wasn't completely awkward as we stood watching the indicator light for the elevator get closer to our floor. After a moment, Bryan said, "Running helps me think. I swear, I do my best problem-solving on the trails and bike paths."

I nodded as if he'd said something profound. "When I run, I mostly think about how much I never want to run again."

Bryan's features softened, and I saw the sliver of a smile form. "That's right. You're all about walking."

I waited for the anger that usually came when he mentioned something from the past, but it didn't come.

The elevator arrived, and he held out his hand to gesture for me to enter first. I stepped in and stood in the opposite corner. "I've been known to traverse the city on foot. I dare anyone to take me on in a walkathon."

"Quite a dare. I'd love to take you on."

I bit back the first thing I thought of to say—which was way too flirty for someone who'd been keeping him at a distance—and looked away.

He drummed his fingers against the elevator bar as the car descended. "Does walking help you think? What do you do to blow off steam or escape or whatever?"

"I go to the movies."

That hung between us as the elevator reached the first floor. The smell of popcorn, the chill of the air conditioner on a hot summer day, the private twilight of the dark theater. As the door opened, he said my name in that smoky voice. "Kat."

There was a pang of remorse in his tone. Instinctively, I took a step closer, all my self-preservation, all my resolutions, falling away at the sound of it.

"What is it?" I asked softly.

"Nothing." He was ice again. He repeated the word as he walked out of his building, and started running the second he hit the sidewalk.

14

BRYAN

Five Years Ago

The waves lapped the shore with the calming rhythm of the night's low tide—a slow sort of whoosh in before the moon pulled the water back out to sea. It was the perfect soundtrack for midnight kissing, and I couldn't get enough of her.

Maybe it had extra punch because I knew it was as far as we'd go, as far as I'd allow myself to go. Not that I didn't want to do everything with her, because I did. *Every. Single. Thing.*

But before anything more happened between us, we needed to be on the up-and-up with everyone, Nate included. I wanted her to be mine officially. For now, though, I was more than thrilled to have her stretched out next to me on a blanket on the sand, and I was glad Nate was keeping busy most evenings, either with prep for his new job or with the occasional date with a woman who worked at the café next to the store.

I pulled Kat to me, kissing her harder and deeper, and she responded by roping her arms around my neck and wriggling her sexy little body closer.

Dangerously close. She slid a leg between mine, and I wanted to yank her under me, pull her down hard on top of me . . . anything. Especially when she started exploring, running her hands over my chest then down to my stomach. I groaned, both happy and frustrated. I loved how she touched me, but I couldn't risk going further.

"We have to be careful, Kat," I said as she reached beneath my T-shirt, spreading her hand across my stomach, her fingers inching toward the waistband of my jeans. "We can't do more than kiss."

"Why?" she asked with a borderline pout.

"Because. Because I'm your brother's friend. Because I'm older than you."

"You're only five years older. And I'm an adult."

"I know. But still," I said, reaching for her hands, hating stopping her but knowing I had to.

"I'm old enough to know what I want."

"I know, and I want it too. But we need to slow down."

She ran her fingers through my hair and buried her face in the crook of my neck, kissing my jawline then buzzing her lips up to my ear, trying to break my control. "Do you really want to slow down?" she whispered.

No. God no. I want to slide your body under mine and

bring you the most intense pleasure.

"No, but we need to," I said, and she silenced me with another kiss, running her free hand over my back and making me shudder. She was so potent to me. One hit and all I wanted was more.

"What about in a few months when I'm in New York?" she asked. "Would we have to slow down then?"

I'd been considering that same question the last few days. She'd be in school in New York, and I'd be working in New York. We had an opportunity, a real chance to make a go of something. Maybe it was crazy, and who knew if we could keep up this intensity, but it seemed crazier to let her go.

"No," I admitted. "We wouldn't."

If a grin could be both wicked and innocent, that was it right there on her beautiful face. "So we'll see each other when I go to NYU?"

"Definitely. Of course we'll see each other. Though my job is going to take me out of town a lot." She looked crestfallen. I pulled her back to me, wanting to reassure her, to let her know how much she'd made a mark on me. "Don't be sad, Kat. I'm totally falling for you, and I don't want to take advantage of you. I like you that much. I like you so much it scares me."

"Don't be scared. I don't bite." Then she nibbled on my collarbone, making me laugh. Making me determined to find a way for us to last. It hadn't escaped me, though, that she hadn't returned or really replied to my *I'm falling for you.*

I tried not to let that bother me, wanting to give

her space and time to say it, if she felt it. God, I hoped she felt it.

We kept on like that, going to the beach at night, working together during the day. She even showed me a sketch for a necklace she planned to create. My time at her house was getting short, and we both knew we'd have to figure out the next step.

At the end of the week, we were at the theater again, the place where we'd first kissed, first admitted we had feelings for each other. After the credits rolled, she grasped my hand tight and looked me in the eyes. "Remember what you said the other night?"

"When you were telling me about a new necklace design?" I teased, hoping I knew the night she meant.

"No." She swatted me lightly on the arm.

"When we discussed the merits of raccoons on film?"

She shook her head. "Not that either."

I rested my index finger on my chin. "Hmm, could it be the night we talked about all the places we want to see in Paris when we go there someday?"

"Not that either. But I definitely want to go to Paris with you."

"And I want to go with you too," I said, squeezing her hand. "So, what's the thing I'm supposed to remember from the other night?"

"When you said you were falling for me," she said in a sweet whisper.

I nodded, my heart beating furiously fast.

She kept her eyes on me, holding my gaze as she spoke. "I'm falling for you too."

15

KAT

Present Day

Bryan went for his run, and I went to the movies. I had plenty of work to do, but I also had a lot of steam to let off.

The cinema around the corner was showing the newest romantic comedy, but I couldn't stomach romance now. I bought a ticket for an action flick. I needed improbable car chases and ridiculously implausible getaways. I slinked down into a seat in the back, leaving the looming pile of homework, necklace orders, and the supply chain issues untouched for the next two hours.

There were only a few other people in the theater for the midafternoon showing on a Thursday. Some solo moviegoers had snagged seats near the front, and there were two pairs of friends in the middle rows.

As the hero hacked into a laptop, I had a thought,

and I followed where it led me. I'd once made a custom necklace for a computer programmer turned bestselling author and had scoured the city for the charms she wanted—floppy disks and motherboards that I cut down to size. The vendor I'd hooked up with had started expanding into other recycled materials, including old tires and worn-out bike chains.

I was the farthest back in the theater, so I broke movie protocol and woke my phone long enough to tap out a reminder to track down the name. Then I guiltily put it away and tried to pay attention to the action on the screen.

But now all I could think about was finding the name of the vendor in my email archive. After another attempt to focus, I apologized to Mr. Gosling and committed my second movie sin of the hour—I got up and left before the end credits.

There was a coffee shop between the theater and the Made Here offices, and I ducked in to grab a something-ccino and some Wi-Fi, settling with my drink and my iPad at a table near the window. Now, when had I made that charm . . .

I stared out the window as I thought back. It was peak afternoon, and the early escapers were beginning to slip out of their offices, and drivers waited in their cars for their riders. A few had their phones out, and one guy across the street looked like he was taking a selfie, just from the way he held the phone up, which was only funny because he was a middle-aged man with a graying flattop.

And it was only because I was watching the selfie

chauffeur that I saw a fit and handsome man in a gray T-shirt and running shorts lope by—he had already passed before my wandering brain realized that it was Bryan coming back from his run. And I still hadn't quite processed that when he jogged back into view going the other way.

A moment later, the café door opened, and Bryan came in, wove through the tables, and stopped in front of mine, hands on his hips. Sweat beaded his brow and darkened his T-shirt. He was breathing deep but not fast, his jaw was tight, and it looked like his run hadn't done much to ease his frustration.

"You're making me crazy," he said in a low voice.

"I am?" I gaped up at him. "Why? I thought the mentorship was going well."

"It is." He dropped into the other chair, still frowning at me. "But you act like nothing happened."

"Like what didn't happen?"

His jaw flexed. "Philly. The factory."

"Nothing did happen in your office in Philly."

He pointed at me like a detective pointing at a suspect. "Aha! You know exactly what I'm talking about. And don't say it was me spilling coffee on my shirt."

That was exactly what I'd been about to say, so I had to think of something else. "Then I don't know what you mean," I lied.

He leaned across the table. And lowered his voice. "We almost kissed."

"Almost is not the same as did," I whispered back, leaning in to mirror him.

"But you *wanted* to. And you knew I wanted to."

"I can't read your mind."

"Some things don't need telepathy." He leaned closer still, his voice going all velvet and gravel. "I bet you know what I'm thinking right now."

Not fair. The way he said it, the way his eyes held my gaze and then lowered to my lips, evoked all our past and present, all the levels on which we knew each other. I bit my lip and he exhaled sharply, leaning back and running his hand through his sweaty hair.

"I called you that day. I emailed you that afternoon. You totally blew me off."

"I went to a show," I said truthfully. "I had my phone in my purse on silent."

He narrowed his eyes at my flimsy—but true—explanation. "I've been trying for weeks to talk to you."

"You've talked to me every day."

"Alone." He motioned between us. "To talk about this. You've been avoiding me."

I sighed. "No, Bryan. I've been avoiding being alone with you."

He seemed startled, either at what I said or that I'd admitted it. "But . . . why? I thought we were getting along great that day. I enjoyed showing you what I was working on and hearing your plans . . ."

"I liked that too."

"And we've been good since then. So, again . . . why?"

"Because we . . ." I copied his motion between us. "We can't be a thing. So there's nothing to talk about."

He thought about his reply a long time. Then he did the same thing he did in his office in Philly, reaching out to tuck my hair behind my ear, lingering just a moment to brush my cheek with his thumb. "That is tragic." He seemed to collect himself and dropped his hand, glancing out the window and then around the café, a lot like I had when I'd snuck a note into my phone in the movie. "But you're right."

I knew I was right. But it sucked to hear him agree.

"We have to appear above reproach," he continued, and my mind snagged on that one word—"appear."

He scooted his chair closer, then pulled my iPad between us as if we were looking at something, heads together. His hand rested on my knee for a moment, then slid away. "If you had taken my call that day, here's what I would have told you went down on that phone call I had." The way we were sitting with our heads together, his voice was only a murmur. "Wilco is suing us for wrongful termination. It's totally ridiculous—he was unquestionably over the line with that intern. But the board wants to play things safe, and I can't take a chance this will blow up in our faces."

"Oh, Bryan." This time I touched his knee under the table. He seemed to need the sympathy of a touch. "I'm so sorry. I read about the firing online, but I had no idea . . ."

"No one does." He covered my hand with his and held it where it was. "No one can know. And that means I can't risk any gossip or rumors, anything that could bite us in the ass. Plus, my board is incredibly conservative." His thumb traced over the back of my hand. "So here we are. I want nothing more than to follow through on what we started, but work and personal can't come within ten feet of each other."

I shivered, but everything inside of me heated up. "Wait. Go back to the part where you want to follow through on what we started."

"I've thought of nothing else. Except for occasional breaks to, you know, run my business so I can pay my employees."

"I'm sure they appreciate it."

I glanced up to find him watching me. He was so dizzyingly near it was as if every nerve ending in my body was exposed, and when he spoke, he breathed across every last one of them.

"I think about you all the time. I think about how beautiful you are and how smart you are and how funny you are, and how I want nothing more than to take you out to the movies and hold your hand and laugh with you. Or laugh at different things. To learn more about what you think is funny. Like, are you pro- or anti-pratfall?"

His eyes were sparkling and playful.

I grinned so wide my face would have hurt, but I didn't think I could feel anything except happiness right now. "I love pratfalls. I love non-sequitur humor, and I love dark humor, and I especially love stupid humor." Was it weird that in the same moment we talked about why we couldn't be a thing, we were suddenly giving in to the temptation to learn everything about each other? "What about you?"

"Cartoon cats and late-night talk shows. I like politics, so I enjoy their political humor. And I'm almost embarrassed to admit this, but my sister Jess loves to send me memes and I laugh at just about any meme with a dog saying some ridiculous thing. Well, in the caption."

"I know how a meme works, Bryan," I teased.

He grinned. "Hey, you asked me if I was going running, while I was standing in my running shoes, five minutes after I said, 'I'm going for a run.' So a little less sass, Captain Obvious."

"Is Jess still in LA?" I asked, remembering his parents had moved there with his younger sister after he started college.

He nodded. "Yes. She's in college now. Premed. Still brilliant, and she's putting herself through school taking photos of celebrities."

"That's right. You once said she had *stars in her eyes.*"

"Yes. That's Jess. She loves movies too."

"What about you? What are your favorite movies?"

"Just in case the guys' committee is listening, I'll tell you *The Fast and The Furious* or *The Hangover.*" Then he lowered his voice and whispered, "But I'll admit to you, only you, that it's actually *Casablanca.*"

Pinch me now, I thought. *Wake me up from this dream.* Because right then I closed my eyes and watched that perfect film unfurl in front of me, a romance that left you breathless no matter how many times you'd seen it. I could feel myself sinking into that heady state, like I was under a spell, transfixed, and I could touch the scenes, feel every sensation the characters felt zip through me.

"They'll always have Paris," I mused. "How can a bittersweet ending be so perfect?"

"Because Rick is thinking of the right thing to do, the right thing for the Resistance and the right thing for—"

He broke off so suddenly that I looked around to see if he'd seen something. Did I have a guilty conscience or what?

I closed my eyes and flashed back to my parents, to the store, to my plans. Then to Professor Oliver, and his wife, and my business. Everything else was much more important than a mere feeling. I just wanted to ignore reality a little longer.

"I could sit here until they close this café, just talking to you," I said.

"That would be nice. But I'd rather take you out to dinner. Then we could walk around the city . . ."

"You know, mentors and mentees have meals together all the time, I'm sure. They have to eat."

"I don't think I could spend an entire evening with you without everyone who looks at us knowing what I'm thinking."

I felt lightheaded, like I'd just taken a painkiller and gotten that warm flush where it kicks in and spreads throughout your chest and belly. The little hairs on my arms were standing on end.

"Definitely too risky," I said.

"Definitely. Not just because of the lawsuit. I don't want anything to look bad for you, or for Made Here, or for the school. But the lawsuit makes me extra paranoid. I didn't even want to email you all the things I've been thinking these past few weeks."

My heart melted. When I looked up at him, his lips were so, so close. "You could call me," I said.

"Tonight?"

I was a pinball machine, buzzing and humming, saying yes, yes, yes. Then I remembered the name of the vendor.

"I would love that. And you may want to try Geeking Out in the Red Hook. Great guys, and super speedy with parts."

He shook his head appreciatively. "Do you have any idea how hot it is that you are this damn business savvy?"

"No. Are we talking broiling, boiling, or scorching?"

"Smoking."

We behaved ourselves, except for some secret smiles, scooting apart once I put my tablet—and the excuse for sitting so close—away.

I didn't want the moment to end, but it wasn't truly ending. We had plans, in a way, for that night.

16

KAT

Present Day

My phone mocked me, a hard brick reminder that I was waiting for a call. I curled deeper into the dented corner of the mustard-colored couch, laptop on my thighs as I worked. Jill was my mirror image, sitting cross-legged on the other end, tapping away on her computer too. Her hair was twisted up and held in place with a red chopstick, and a few dark-blonde strands framed her face. "Finished!"

"Did you finally master Candy Crush?"

"Why, yes, I did. I also finished my list of recommendations for my group of Upper East Side mommies on their training and diet for the next few weeks before the New York City Marathon." Jill was making headway as an actress, but she still took on jobs on the side as a running coach. She operated a few running clinics and clubs, especially for men and women who wanted to tackle marathons for the first time, as well as 5Ks and 10Ks.

"And I deserve a kombucha, but we have none, and that makes me sad."

"Gross. But to each her own."

"Kombucha makes me strong."

"Kombucha makes me gag, but here you go."

I stretched my arm out to the coffee table, grabbed Jill's wallet, and tossed it to her. She caught it in one hand, placed her laptop on the couch, and went on an expedition to the nearest Whole Foods.

I wandered into the kitchen and reached for an apple inside the three-tiered silver-looking wire basket that hung by the side of the kitchen sink. I only kept it because it reminded me of the one towering with fruit—apples, oranges, nectarines, and lemons that threatened to spill out—that my parents had in our home in Connecticut. I washed the apple and then headed into the living room, where I sat on the windowsill and took a bite.

This probably sounded crazy, but my parents really are *that couple*. As in those people you can't believe still love each other madly after all these years. They've been together for thirty years, and my mom still makes breakfast for him every morning. She'll set the table with the same green-and-white checkered plates and the same matching cloth napkins that we've had since I was in high school. Then Dad will come downstairs, give her a kiss on the cheek, and they'll have breakfast together. He'll do the dishes and clean up, and they'll walk to the store holding hands. It's lovely.

When my mom admitted earlier tonight on the phone that the online daily deal had bombed, my heart withered a bit for them. "I'm so sorry, Mom."

"Well, you know, you'll just have to keep me stocked in chocolate, my Katerina."

"I will. I promise. Even though I know it won't come to that."

I took another bite of the apple, thinking of them. When my phone finally rang, I pounced on it.

"Hello?"

"Hey. It's Bryan."

My heart leaped. I was the girl in high school waiting for the quarterback to call. Fine, I'd never dated a football player, and I didn't even care for most sports. But I bet the zing I felt was precisely the same.

"Hey. What are you up to?"

"Talking to you."

I rolled my eyes even though he couldn't see me. Now we really sounded like teenagers again.

"Same to you," I said as I placed the half-eaten apple on the coffee table.

"What'd you do tonight?"

I gave him the rundown, then asked the same of him.

"Work, work, and more work. I heard back from the city of Paris on the padlocks. They said they're trying to make some arrangements for a deal, so that's good. But the best part is this amazingly brilliant

MBA student I'm working with may have saved the day for us."

I bounced on my toes. "Really? Did Geeking Out come through?"

"They're putting a competitive bid together tonight. I should have it first thing in the morning, but they said they could meet the timeline."

"Damn. I rock."

"You totally and completely rock."

"Where are you right now?" I asked as I walked down the hall to my bedroom. I didn't know when Jill would return with her kombucha, but I didn't want to be interrupted.

"My apartment. Finally. Car just dropped me off."

"Calling me was the first thing you did when you got home? Nice."

"I walked in two minutes ago."

"I don't even know where you live." I shut the door to my bedroom and lay down on my bed. The one luxury I afforded myself was the bedding. A shimmery purple duvet covered the bed, with pillows in rich shades of red and dark blue.

"Sixtieth and Park."

I wanted to whistle in admiration. I pictured the block perfectly, seeing it on a rain-soaked night, the quiet street glistening, lined with beautiful brick brownstones. He probably lived in one of those buildings. Double doors, four stories, hardwood floors, white-paned windows that opened onto the kind of street that romantic comedy heroines strolled down, holding hands with their lovers.

"What's on tap the rest of the night? More work?"

"I'm calling it a night on the work front. No more email, no more reports. I'm just kicking back on my couch talking to this girl with my cell phone pressed against my head. I'm probably getting a brain tumor, but c'est la vie."

"You're not one of those AirPod people? You haven't been walking around like an Apple commercial all evening?"

"Hey now! I lost my AirPods," he admitted a little sheepishly. "Three pairs."

I laughed. Something about a man who made cuff links and tie clips losing his AirPods hit me in the funny bone. "Your Achilles' heel."

"They are my downfall, yes. Anyway, now that you've finagled my AirPod secret from me, what else do you want to know?"

I shifted onto my side and played with the tassel on one of my purple pillows. What did I want to know about Bryan? "I got it. Shoes on airplanes. On or off?"

"On, of course. As if I would ever take my shoes off on a plane."

"Totally agree. Why do people do that? Stretch their big stinky feet out in front of them and even walk up and down the aisles without their shoes."

"I'm telling you, there should be a regulation against removing shoes on planes. And from clipping your nails in public."

"That definitely seems like a health code violation to me."

"You know what I like to do on planes?"

"No. What?"

"Sometimes I go a little wild and leave my cell phone on."

"It doesn't work up there."

"Right, but instead of turning it off when we take off, I just go crazy and leave it on silent. And then I like to see how far up we can go before it stops getting messages, and then I like to see how high we are when it starts picking them up again on the way down."

"You renegade."

"I know, Kat. I'm not afraid to be a bad boy like that."

"Are you though? A bad boy?"

He didn't answer right away. He must have been weighing the question and what I really meant. I wasn't even sure what I really meant. "Do you want me to be a bad boy?"

I rested my head on the pile of pillows. "I don't know," I answered honestly. "I just want you to be yourself."

"I am. With you, I am definitely myself."

That was one of the best compliments I could imagine anyone giving me. From Bryan, it was even better.

We talked like we had five years to catch up on, talked about everything and nothing until I couldn't stop yawning. And finally, we said good night.

"Sweet dreams, Kat."

How could they be anything but sweet?

17

Bryan: Good morning.

Kat: My morning is indeed excellent so far. How is yours?

Brian: I don't think I can top "excellent." What does that involve? Birds making your bed? Mice bringing your slippers?

Kat: Are you implying I'm some kind of princess?

Bryan: Only the good kind. A postmillennial self-rescuing kick-ass princess.

Bryan: With superpowers.

Bryan: And a talking horse.

Kat: Better quit while you're ahead.

Bryan: I'm not a quitter, but I'm not stupid either, so . . . changing the subject. Did you sleep well?

Kat: I did. But I dreamed I walked around New York City all night. Or maybe I actually sleepwalked around New York City. I think I stopped at a bakery and picked up a carrot cake.

Brian: Please tell me that if you sleepwalked all over this city, you did not do it to get a carrot cake.

Kat: Well, not specifically to get the cake. That was incidental.

Bryan: Then tell me it was something besides carrot cake.

Kat: Because carrot is something that should never go in cake?

Bryan: Exactly.

Kat: So maybe it was a nightmare about carrot cake.

Bryan: Let's not talk about nightmares. Let's talk about dreams.

Kat: Fine. I slept perfectly and had very sweet dreams.

Brian: My dreams were anything but sweet.

Kat: Aw, poor baby.

Bryan: I didn't say they weren't good dreams.

Kat: Oh. So they were sweet dirty dreams?

Bryan: They were definitely on the dirtier side.

Kat: Do I want to ask what they were about?

Bryan: Depends. Do you want to know what they were about?

Kat: How would I know that until I know?

Bryan: I'll help you out. If you want me to say they were about you, you want to ask.

Kat: I guess that is the question. Do I want you to say me?

Bryan: I feel like this is going in a "Who's on First?" direction.

Kat: For the record, I find "Who's on First?" hilarious.

Bryan: Noted.

Kat: But not before coffee.

Bryan: I wouldn't do that to you, Kat. I'm not a barbarian.

Kat: What, not even a little bit?

Bryan: Maybe if you ask nicely.

Kat: Hey, Bryan . . . I absolutely want you to say me.

18

KAT

Present Day

Bryan was a fortune-teller. Over the next month, Wilco filed his wrongful termination suit against Made Here, Bryan's board freaked out about it, and we were the absolute model of a mentor and protégé. I knew the Wilco thing was bothering him, though, not because he was worried about the lawsuit, but because he thought he knew the guy. They'd been business partners for years, and Wilco had betrayed him twice: once with his behavior and again with the lawsuit.

It was one of the many things we talked about on the phone. We talked more on the phone in a month than I might have in my whole life—not counting the parents, which should not count.

We met once a week on purpose at the coffee shop where we'd met serendipitously the first time. Once mentor-protégé talk was done, we'd discuss life—ours and in general—and talk about his sister, my brother, the movies, the theater, living in New York. Sometimes we'd argue about what was funny and what wasn't. I suspected he took the opposite opinion from mine to keep things interesting.

And we flirted sometimes. He'd give a little innuendo, and I'd react accordingly. Or sometimes not—to keep things interesting.

We met there on the day we had an appointment for our midterm check-in with Professor Oliver. Bryan had tried again to predict my coffee order, but I'd kept him on his toes. "Come on, Bryan," I teased. "Admit I'm not that predictable."

He shook his head stubbornly. "I'm going to get it eventually. Who'd have thought you'd be so hard to pin down?"

I caught his smirk at the end there and answered in the same spirit. "You're bigger and stronger than I am, so it wouldn't be that hard."

Groaning, he held the door for me as we left the shop. "You're killing me, Kat."

It was a lovely day—the sun was out and it wasn't too cool or too muggy, so I wasn't surprised when Bryan gestured up the street. "You want to walk?"

"Of course." I smirked at him. "Some of us are used to our feet taking us where we want to go."

He held up his hands. "I concede. You win this round."

We set off toward campus. When Bryan had first started working, we'd walk everywhere when I came to visit him—though we'd strolled then, and now we strode purposefully like proper New Yorkers. The more time I spent with Bryan now, the less anger and instead the more confusion I felt when I thought about the breakup. I'd enjoyed seeing New York with him, and I'd thought he'd enjoyed himself too. I wasn't brave enough to ask him about it though. If his explanation—if he had one—made me angry, it would be back to awkward AF working with him. If he melted my heart, that would cause problems, too, because we absolutely could not have a relationship.

In his office on campus, Professor Oliver pulled three chairs into a circle. Bryan and I sat next to each other, inches apart, our eyes never straying from Oliver.

"Ms. Harper, tell me about the business challenges you've weighed in on at Made Here."

"I've been able to devise solutions for some of the supply chain complications that have arisen, from new time frames to replacement suppliers," I said, and then shared more of the details of the projects we'd worked on.

Bryan jumped in. "I can't underestimate the value of this input, Professor. For instance, Ms. Harper's swift and well-researched recommendation for a new vendor single-handedly allowed us to stay on track with one of our key accounts."

Professor Oliver beamed, then asked more questions, which we took turns answering. When the meeting was done, Bryan and I left together, exchanging a high five like we had pulled off some kind of caper, when all we'd done was told the truth—and omitted the part where we'd dreamed of each other at night.

As we reached the street, Bryan's phone buzzed. "It's Caldwell—one of our board members. I just need to take this quickly."

He stepped a few feet away, and as I reached for my phone to check my messages, I nearly bumped into a middle-aged man with a graying flattop.

"Sorry!" I said, and the man continued on his way without acknowledging the bump or my apology. Too busy on his phone to walk properly maybe.

But something made me stop and watch him go. He seemed familiar. I just couldn't place it.

"Everything okay?" Bryan asked when his call ended and he came over to me.

"Yeah. I saw someone who I thought I recognized. But I can't think from where."

He looked down the street and then back at me. "It's a big city full of a lot of people. Some of them are bound to look familiar."

* * *

We'd definitely gotten into a habit. I wasn't sure I could sleep half as well without our nightly phone calls.

"Confession time," Bryan said. "What were you thinking during the meeting today?"

I'd just put a second coat of scarlet polish on my

toes and was feeling a little scarlet myself. "Honestly?" I asked.

"Always."

"I was thinking about crawling under the table."

He choked like I'd caught him when he was drinking. "You naughty girl," he growled.

I said as sweetly as I could, "Well, there was a paper clip, you see. I didn't want to just leave it there."

"Uh-huh."

"I wouldn't want the cleaning crew to vacuum it up and damage their equipment."

"Sure. You were just thinking it would be a quick cleanup job."

I gasped. "You think it was another kind of job?"

"God, I hope it was another kind of job."

"What kind of job did you have in mind?" I purred.

"I think you know."

"Do I?"

"You wouldn't say it in that sex-kitten voice if you didn't know."

I smiled even though he couldn't see it. "Hmm. Maybe I'll turn it around and ask you what you were thinking about."

"I believe I just told you."

"Good thing I'm *always* ready to pitch in and do the dirty work."

19

BRYAN

Five Years Ago

On her visits to New York after I started work there, Kat and I explored the city together. I'd lived there while in college and grad school, but it was different with Kat, treading the sidewalks and weaving ourselves into the fabric of the city. We wandered through the Metropolitan Museum, kissed in front of the fountain at Lincoln Center, and held hands as we meandered in and out of Manhattan's neighborhoods.

I wanted more than kisses, so much more, and so did she, but we'd agreed to wait till she moved to the city and was ready to start college. But there was something electric about anticipation too. Knowing you're not going there—yet—but both of you knowing it's within arm's reach.

As we strolled along a tree-lined street in the Village one weekend, I subtly guided her in the direction I wanted to go, without making it look like I was steering her. When we got near, though, I told her I had a surprise.

She arched an eyebrow, but her eyes sparkled. "What kind of surprise?"

"If I tell you, it won't be a surprise, now will it? We're almost there."

"Oh!" She stopped in her tracks. "I forgot. I have exciting news."

"What is it?"

"There's a little boutique owner in Mystic who likes my necklaces. She asked me to join her at an upcoming festival in town and try selling some at a booth," she said, bouncing with excitement.

"How could you forget to tell me that? That's huge, Kat. I'm so happy for you." I pulled her in close for a hug. "You haven't even started school yet, and you're already on your way to being a star."

"I'm hardly a star," she said, then planted a quick kiss on my lips. "But it's a start."

I reached for her hand. "It's the start of amazing things for you."

Soon we reached a tiny vintage shop, everything slightly rustic, slightly pastel, very French. I'd stumbled upon this place a while ago, but forgot about it, since it wasn't really my thing. Then I'd remembered it because of Kat, knowing it was perfect for her. "This is your surprise."

She arched an eyebrow. "You want me to become a consignment clothing fan? I'm not opposed. Just surprised you'd take such an interest in my style."

"I'm not trying to change your style. Just go in. You'll see."

Once inside, she was the proverbial kid in the candy store, wide-eyed and slack-jawed when she saw the display of Paris-themed jewelry, bracelets, and necklaces. She loved all things Paris, and I'd had a hunch she'd be taken in by the Eiffel Tower, beret, and baguette charms.

I smiled as I watched her take it all in. Seeing her happy was like a drug. I'd do whatever I could to get this reaction from my girl. "I thought you might get a kick out of it. Especially now that you're getting requests for your necklaces."

She reached for me and wrapped her hand around my arm. "I love it. Paris and I, we have a lifelong kind of thing going on."

"Good. Pick anything you like." Fine, it wasn't Tiffany's, and I wasn't some loaded hedge fund manager with the money to shop at Tiffany's. But judging from the way Kat's brown eyes seemed to twinkle, I might as well have brought her to Aladdin's cave, full of gems and rubies. I ran my hand along her lower back, unable to resist touching her. She sighed and inched closer to me as she checked out necklaces and rings. She held up a ring with a fleur-de-lis that she liked, showing it to me.

"Cute," I murmured as I brushed my lips against her neck. I slipped my hand under the back of her shirt, tracing her soft skin. "You feel so good," I whispered.

"You're distracting me," she said, but she moved

closer too. I wanted to tug her into my arms, thread my fingers through her hair, and kiss her deeply right in the store.

The woman behind the counter cleared her throat, and that was my cue to keep it PG. Kat picked out a fleur-de-lis charm lined with purple stones to make it sparkle.

"Wait for me outside," I told her, then went to the register to pay for the gifts.

A minute later I left the store, tucking a tiny white bag into my wallet. I'd save what was inside for the next time I saw her, but I had the Eiffel Tower necklace I'd picked out in my hand and asked Kat to turn around. She lifted up her hair, and I kissed her lightly on her neck, savoring that sweet, sexy moment when she shivered under my touch. "I could do this all day," I said as I fastened the necklace.

"Put jewelry on me?" she teased.

"No. Kiss you," I said, then kissed my way to her ear as she pressed her body against me. "I love kissing you. I'm so crazy for you. And I know this is just a little necklace, but I wanted you to have something from me. Something you liked."

She turned around, looping her arms around my neck. "I love it, Bryan. I totally *love* it."

That word burrowed into my heart, and I wanted to say it, to tell her all that I felt for her. But I kept it back for now. She had the world ahead of her, and I didn't want to rush a thing.

"Let's go walk around NYU. You're going to be there in just a few weeks."

We wandered over to campus, and she peered in the buildings, checking out dorms and classrooms, vibrating with excitement. "I can't believe I'm going to be here soon. It's going to be amazing. Did you love it here?"

"Absolutely. Every second of it," I said. "College is everything they say it is."

"What do you mean?"

"It's the time when you find yourself. When you figure out what you want."

"Sounds intimidating." Her grin made me doubt that anything intimidated her.

"Intimidating and a hell of a lot of fun if you find the right balance."

"I can't wait to start."

As we reached the campus bookstore, my phone chimed with an email. When I slid my finger across the screen and saw who it was from, I held up my finger and signaled to Kat, saying, "I'll be right back. I need to see what my boss wants. I'll meet you in the store."

I clicked open the email, and the subject line read *Paris*. That was some weird synchronicity, considering where we'd just been shopping.

Looks like there might be an opening soon in our Paris office. You're fluent, right? Let's talk Monday about this.

20

KAT

Present Day

After a caffeine-fueled night of studying, I powered through a brutal, caffeine-fueled test in one of my courses. When I filed the exam at the end of the class, submitting it from my laptop, I felt good about how I'd done. I was less worried about my marks than I was about proving what I'd learned. Maybe someday I could turn My Favorite Mistakes into a business like Made Here, with a board, stockholders, employees, and revenues with many, many zeros.

Optimistic about my prospects, I headed down the wide wooden staircase to the first floor and pushed open the door into the late-October air.

Fall had coasted into Manhattan, bringing with it the crisp air and short splash of gold and red leaves on the trees in the parks. I looped my orange scarf with white stars around my neck and pushed on a pair of champagne-colored sunglasses to block the bright midday rays. My brown boots clicked against the sidewalk as I checked the time on my phone. I had a meeting with Claire Oliver in an hour. She'd finally reached back out to me and asked me to meet her at the café at the Met, adding that since she and her husband were avid supporters of the museum, she had other meetings there too.

On the subway I checked my phone for messages. It was habit any time I stayed in one place long enough, because Bryan and I had become regular texters.

To my delight I found a message waiting from him.

Bryan: Breakfast of champions.

He'd sent me a photo of French toast.

Kat: Whoa. That is some Instagram-level breakfast photography. Is there nothing you can't do?

Bryan: Shh. Don't tell anyone. It's my fallback profession.

Kat: A breakfast food influencer? Depends on what magic you can work with an avocado and poached egg.

. . .

A few seconds later, an image popped up of just that, but the angle was more odd than artistic.

Kat: The idea that you are somewhere in this city surreptitiously capturing a snap of someone else's breakfast delights me.

I was rewarded with a shot of home fries.

Bryan: I can't stop! I've gone down the food photo rabbit hole.

Kat: More, more! Show me some . . . blueberries.

A minute later, that was the image that landed on my phone.

Bryan: See? I can do commissions too. Impressive, isn't it?

Kat: So impressive I can hardly believe I know you. You've got skills.

Bryan: Sadly, I also have a food craving now. I want blueberries.

Kat: Don't deny yourself. Go for it.

Bryan: You are such an enabler.

Kat: You say that like it's a bad thing.

Bryan: Also, you should be having breakfast with me.

Kat: Breakfast is one of my three favorite meals.

Bryan: Long slow clap.

Bryan: Also, breakfast is awesome.

Bryan: Breakfast is proof we were meant to be morning people.

Kat: Lies, vicious lies. I am a night owl, and I'll fight anyone to prove it, as long as it's after noon.

Bryan: My illusions are shattered. I'm not sure I can continue this conversation when we disagree on such important matters.

We couldn't stop texting, and we kept up the volley as I left the train and walked up the steps of the museum, hoping in some ways we'd never stop.

* * *

"I showed these around to some buyers I know, and everyone is in love with your necklaces. They think they could be the next big thing," Claire said, looking very *now* in a short red linen dress that I'd seen last year's best actress winner wearing while shopping on Melrose Avenue in the pages of *Us* magazine.

"I'm so pleased to hear that, Mrs., er . . . Claire." I quickly corrected myself, and she nodded in approval when I used her first name. We sat in the café, drinking afternoon tea in white china cups with a delicately painted green vine circling the rim. I set mine in its saucer and ventured forward, hoping this information was why she'd called me. "I'd love to know more about the buyers, and who they're buying for."

She grinned like a Cheshire cat, then mentioned two names. The first was a distributor that supplied to the trendiest independent boutiques on the East Coast, and the second worked for one of the largest and hippest department store chains in the country—Elizabeth's. The chain was helmed by the reclusive and rarely seen Elizabeth Mortimer, whose mother, also named Elizabeth, had started the first store in Seattle many years ago, then steadily expanded across the country. Elizabeth's taste was legendary, a cocktail of trendy and timeless. She stayed entirely out of the limelight, though, letting her stores and their displays do the talking.

I leaned back in my chair, gobsmacked. "Let me just catch my breath."

Claire's smile switched to a more neutral expression. "The only thing is, we'd like to see more variety."

As a critique, it was hardly bad, but it wasn't the compliment I'd hoped for. But I was more worried about "the only thing is," which rarely preceded anything good.

"Did you have something in mind?" I asked cautiously.

"As a matter of fact, I do. I wondered if you'd consider moving beyond the idea of favorite mistakes to include, quite simply, favorites. We thought that might broaden your base. And we all seem most fond of your European stylings, and were hoping to see more in that vein—European Favorites."

"There could be My Favorite Mistakes and also My Favorites?"

"I rather like the sound of that."

"I can do that. I can definitely do that." I started flashing back to my time in Paris, then flicking ahead to the quirky little design blogs I visited each night. I'd need to cobble together my own style, of course. But inspiration often comes from collecting ideas and transforming them into something unique. Like from art, I mused, thinking about my current setting— surrounded by one of the greatest collections of art the world has ever known. "When would you and the buyers want to see them?"

"Soon. Very soon. I think we can get your designs into their stores if we can mix up the look, and I really want to get them in for the holiday season. Which isn't that far away. We have our holiday marketing in place already and have for months, but we'd love to find a true standout for the season. Just the right style to focus on for holiday jewelry." She steepled her fingers together. The look drawn across her porcelain skin and fine features revealed nothing.

I nodded several times. "I better get started," I said, and I didn't have to feign enthusiasm. The "only thing" wasn't that bad after all.

"Actually, Kat. I haven't even gotten to the proposition part yet."

"Oh. Okay." I took a drink of my tea and waited.

She placed her hands flat on the table, her diamond ring catching the light. "Is My Favorite Mistakes open for a small seed investment?"

I nearly choked on my tea. I coughed a few times, and I could feel my face turning red as I hacked at the fancy table in the fancy café in the fancy museum. "Excuse me?"

"I want to be an angel investor. Think of it as expansion capital to fund the new design work."

"Right. Yes. Of course. Absolutely. I'll do it right now." I was so bowled over I could barely form words.

"Is that a yes?" Claire seemed on the cusp of annoyed.

I collected myself. "I would be thrilled. I would be absolutely thrilled to have you as an investor."

When she shared the amount, it took all I had not to jump out of my chair and victory dance. Never in my wildest dreams had I imagined having an investor.

"Now, the money is to be allocated solely to the business. You can't use it to pay your rent or anything like that." She wagged a finger at me and narrowed her eyes. She was being playful, but she was also serious. Given her tone, I felt compelled to respond with a salute.

"Absolutely."

"And I do have some stipulations."

"Of course."

"First, you need to finish your MBA. I'm a big believer in the value of education, so even if this helps your business take off, you must finish your degree. Or else I'll need the money paid back."

"Totally. I'm definitely finishing my degree. I'm so committed I'm beyond committed."

"Second, after you finish your degree and can focus solely on the business, I'll put another round into My Favorite Mistakes at the same multiple."

My heart sang. Everything seemed possible.

"Great."

"Third, when we first met, you mentioned the markets in Paris and all the little trinkets and charms to be had there for a steal. Then my buyers mentioned they preferred your European stylings, and I started thinking . . ."

21

KAT

Present Day

"Paris, Mom! She wants to send me to Paris. And it's a requirement."

I was on the steps of the museum, my hand cupped over my mouth even though I wasn't truly trying to keep my voice down. How could I?

"That is wonderful."

"She's like a fairy godmother. And she's making me, Mom, *making me* go to Paris as part of the investment. To find vendors to expand my designs. Can you please just pinch me now because I must be dreaming!"

A group of school kids chattered noisily as they raced down the sprawling steps to the hot dog carts and pretzel vendors on Fifth Avenue. A guy with a salt-and-pepper flattop gave me a once-over as he passed, and I tensed, thinking of the man I'd seen on the NYU campus who looked unplaceably familiar. I turned and scanned for him again, but he was already pushing through the revolving doors.

I blew out the breath I'd held. Was I seriously worried about a guy who reminded me of a guy who reminded me of someone else? In a city with the population of New York, that confirmed madness.

Pushing him out of my mind, I returned my focus to the call. "I'm going to use some of the investment for the trip and to buy the supplies. But if the buyers pick up my designs, then I'll ramp up the business quickly, and I can help pay off your loan for Mystic Landing with my revenue."

"Katerina, I've told you to stop worrying about us."

"Mom, I want to do this. Just let me help. I mean, I know I don't have the money yet, but I will soon. And nothing would make me happier than helping you guys."

"Pfft. Enough. Tell me more about your trip to Paris. That's what I really want to hear."

I shared more of the details, told her I'd come out to visit before I left, and then said goodbye. I looked around at all the people streaming in and out of the museum, then up at the darkening sky. I shook my head in amazement. I was still giddy and didn't think I'd come down from this high for a long time, nor did I want to. I wanted to share it with someone else. Someone special.

Bryan answered on the second ring. "Hey," he said in a sweet voice he used just for me.

"I have amazing news. Where are you right now?"

"Just finished up a meeting on the Upper East Side."

"I'm at the Met right now. About to do some work on a new expansion project for My Favorite Mistakes, and I thought perhaps my mentor might want to join me for a few minutes. It's a business meeting, of course."

"I'll be there in ten."

* * *

The morning light reflected off Monet's water lilies. The brushstrokes from the Impressionist master made me think about shapes, colors, and new ways of looking.

"I'm thinking I should totally add a line of water lily charms to My Favorite Mistakes."

Bryan played along as we strolled past paintings. He wore slate-gray pants and a green-and-white checkered shirt with recycled bike chain cuff links. Completing the look was a tie that I longed to unknot. "While you're at it, why not throw in some haystacks too?" He tipped his head to another Monet. "Your favorite painting, right?"

My heart stuttered at the realization that he hadn't forgotten the last time we were here five years ago. From the caramel macchiatos to the Eiffel Tower to haystacks, he'd held on to so many details of me. My heart felt bigger and fuller. "You remember?"

He shot me a smile, then nodded. "Yes, I remember."

I wanted to wrap my arms around him and kiss him, but I resisted. "Maybe I should get some of those melty clocks like in a Dalí."

"Or how about just a bunch of drip mark charms from a Pollock? Because I would have to think drip marks would qualify as favorite mistakes."

We stopped to sit on a blond hardwood bench in the middle of the gallery, keeping necessary space between us. But when he rested a hand on the bench and I did the same, only six inches separated us, or we might have been holding hands.

I glanced at his fingers and restrained the impulse to lace them through mine. Another reason the Met was beautiful to me just then—I could be tempted, but couldn't give in to the moment. There were too many people around us—tourists and school kids, couples and families.

"When do you think you'll go to Paris?"

"Two weeks maybe. Claire and I even looked up flights during our chat. If I go over Veteran's Day weekend, I won't have to miss too many classes."

He lowered his voice but looked straight ahead. "Speaking of missing, I'll miss you when you're gone."

My stomach flipped. I wanted to brush my lips against his, to run my hand over his arm. To let him tuck a strand of my hair behind my ear. I could see him doing it so tenderly. "Same here," I said.

"Kat."

There was something new in his voice. Something softer, more vulnerable. Something like love perhaps? My heart trembled with hope at the possibility. I ached for him to feel the same way that I did. I was falling for him again, and I couldn't bear the thought of another rejection. I hadn't said a word about my feelings this time, so I might walk away with a shred of dignity, but not with my heart whole. Even with the rules, even unable to touch, I was all in.

He shifted gears back to bantering. "So, you're going to Paris, you're going to find new designs and make more necklaces and be a superstar. You won't let success change you though, right?"

"Ha. I honestly just want to make enough money from My Favorite Mistakes to help out my parents. Mystic Landing isn't doing well."

"I didn't know. You hadn't mentioned that."

I shrugged. "I'm pretty good at keeping some things buttoned up."

"Tell me what's going on. Maybe I can help. I do know a thing or two about running a business." He held up his thumb and forefinger to show a sliver of space.

I gave him the rundown and sighed when I'd filled him in. "They've been trying everything to drive more traffic to the store. If I can help them pay off the loan, they can have some breathing room, you know? Things have got to pick up soon. I just want to buy them some time."

"Hmm."

"Hmm, what?"

He stared at a Monet again, but he wasn't looking at the painting. I could see the wheels turning in his head. "It might not be a traffic issue."

"But there aren't as many customers."

"Right. But maybe the solution isn't in driving in more traffic. Sometimes it's something else."

"Well, let me know when you figure out what that is."

"Would it be okay with you if I visited the store?"

I furrowed my brow. He couldn't be serious. "You would do that?"

"Of course. I'd love to just take a look around and see if I can come up with an idea. Their daughter, Kat, is my protégé after all. It seems like the right thing to do," he said, and leaned a tiny bit closer to me without touching.

"That would be above and beyond the call of duty."

"Consider it done, Kat." Then he said my name again as if it were a strange object he'd never seen. "Kat. What's the story with Kat? Your parents didn't actually name you that, did they?"

"Like that's so implausible?"

"It's like a writer's name. A made-up name. It has to be short for something."

"Didn't my brother ever tell you?"

"Never."

"Guess, then."

"Ah, so it is short for something?"

I nodded.

"Let me think. If I guess wrong, I don't want to be the same wrong as everyone else. I bet most people go for the obvious—Katherine, Kathleen, or Kathy."

"They do."

"And then they guess Katie or Kaitlin."

"Those are very popular guesses." I enjoyed watching him work through the question and couldn't keep the Mona Lisa smile from my face.

"Then maybe something farther afield, like Katrina or Katya."

"Katya?" I raised my brows. "I don't get that one as much."

The gold flecks in his forest-green eyes shimmered with playfulness. I knew he was reading my reactions to his attempts—I'd taken the same class in business school—but it was as thrilling as ESP to have his attention focused on me. "But I don't think any of those are right." He leaned his shoulder closer to me. "You're Katerina."

He pulled away to gauge my reaction, which I didn't try to hide. Grinning, he brushed imaginary dirt off his shoulder. "I impress myself sometimes."

"You impressed me. I've never told anyone my full name, and haven't used it."

"Really?"

"My mom always wanted me to be Kat. My dad said I needed a real name, so they named me Katerina. But no one ever called me that. I've always been Kat. Funny, because now my mom calls me Katerina."

"Kat is a perfect name for you. But so is Katerina. Did you ever think about using it?"

I shrugged my shoulders. "I'm used to Kat. After you've gone through all the teasing, it becomes a badge of honor when you get older—that you made it through middle school with people saying, 'Here, kitty, kitty' or 'Cat got your tongue?'"

Bryan laughed once. "Or 'Josie and the Pussycats.'"

I shot him a curious look. "I don't get that one often."

He downshifted his volume. "My bad. I was thinking of pussycats."

My brows climbed. "Aren't you Captain Innuendo today?"

"Just today?" He leaned in closer. "True or false: I'm thinking of pussycats right now."

I rolled my eyes. "You're the worst."

"Maybe," he murmured in my ear, "I'm thinking of you and all the things I want to do to you right now."

"We are in a museum," I said in an outraged whisper.

"Just saying." He wiggled his eyebrows.

"We're not doing anything here," I said primly.

He shrugged. "A man has dreams. He has all kinds of dirty dreams."

"Oh, really?" I wanted to know his sweet dreams and his dirty ones. "When do you have racy dreams?"

"Often."

I took the bait. "*How* often?"

"All night." He breathed deep as if taking in the scent of my hair. "All day."

"So . . . a daydream, then."

"Exactly. Like now." I glanced at him, and he took my breath away the way he looked at me with such wanting. "I'm daydreaming of you . . . tasting you, kissing you, touching you."

"That does sound like a nice dream."

"It's not nice, Kat. It's naughty."

I lowered my voice too, but less breathy, more throaty. "How naughty?"

"On a scale of one to ten?" he asked, eyes on my lips. "Five hundred."

I smiled. "That's off the charts."

"And off the map," he said, tapping the brochure with the layout of the museum that I still held. "Because in my mind, I'm grabbing your hand"—he covered my hand with his—"then taking you to a dark corner and doing dirty things to you."

I can't say I didn't want that. But I also knew we weren't there yet, and hearing about it was very enticing. "Your ideas intrigue me, Mr. Leighton, but I hardly think the Impressionist gallery is the proper place."

"True. We'd be philistines then."

I laughed. "No one wants to be philistines."

He leaned closer, then whispered, "But it's just the right place to linger with you, innuendo, and the Monets."

"The Monets and I thank you very much."

And my restraint didn't thank me, but my brain did as I stood up. We spent the next couple of hours wandering through the museum, past seascapes and portraits, then Egyptian relics and stone horses.

It was among the Egyptian relics that I noticed him glancing behind him restlessly. "What's wrong?" I asked. "Not nervous about mummies, are you?"

"No." He rubbed his chin with his palm. "See that guy over there?"

I caught where he was pointing, and then turned

as if I was just taking in the splendor of ancient Egypt. My stomach sank as I saw who he must mean. Middle-aged gray flattop.

"I see him," I said tightly.

"I think he's following me," Bryan said between gritted teeth.

I shook my head as fear snaked over me. "No. He's following us."

22

KAT

Present Day

When I showed up at Made Here's offices to work, I spent most of the time with Nicole Blazer in design. She showed me the new line of tie clips with the gold tints I'd suggested, then remarked that she was going to get one for her partner. "She likes to wear the pants in the relationship. And the ties," Nicole said, as we looked at the first set of clips spread out on the coffee table in her office. I felt a pang of jealousy for Nicole and her partner, simply because they weren't a secret, because they were something. They were an unsecret.

"Which one do you like?"

"I love them all. But especially this one." I chose a clip that shone with the gold of a sunset.

"My favorite too! And Bryan loves that one as well," Nicole said, then called out to Bryan, who was walking by her office. "Kat has the best taste."

"She does," he said, flashing something close to, but not quite his normal smile. But no knowing looks, secret winks, or anything personal before he left the doorway.

"He's just stressed about the . . ." Nicole let her voice trail off. The lawsuit was affecting the whole atmosphere at Made Here. No one wanted to talk about Wilco, but the problems he was making for the company were on everyone's mind.

They were certainly on my mind—I was flinching at shadows and seeing familiar faces everywhere. I remembered this feeling too well from my breakup with Michael. And Bryan had pulled back, less worried about reputations or the board's opinion now, and more that his friendship with me had put me in Wilco's line of sight if he got really vindictive. I didn't want that either, but I also didn't want Bryan to shut me out and take this stress on himself. We were friends, I hoped, aside from anything else, and I missed him.

I looked briefly at Bryan as he walked away. I turned back to Nicole, and saw she'd followed my gaze.

"Do you?" she asked, shifting her eyes down the hall. She didn't have to finish the question for me to know what she meant. *Do you like him?*

"No. Of course not. I mean, not like that."

She stood up and shut her door. "You're blushing."

I put a hand on my cheek. Stupid red cheeks. I didn't say anything.

"Hey. It's okay."

I shook my head, as if I could rid myself of all that wanting, hoping, falling. I picked up another tie clip and examined it as if it were a long-lost archaeological relic. "This one is nice too," I added, doing my best to focus on everything except waiting for Bryan.

* * *

That night I sent him a text.

Kat: Hey. You doing okay?

Bryan: I've been better. How are you?

Kat: I am fine, but I am worried about you. I can tell you're stressed.

Bryan: Nah. I'm cool, calm, and as relaxed as an ocean breeze.

Kat: Yeah, right.

Bryan: Seriously though. I appreciate you checking in. I wish this situation were different.

I wasn't entirely sure which situation he meant—our personal situation or the company's. They were all knotted together, so I supposed it didn't matter. And the answer I gave applied in any case.

Kat: I wish it were too.

Bryan: Sweet dreams, Kat.

Kat: Sweet dreams to you. I can tell you need them.

Bryan: I'm going to do everything in my power to dream of you.

23

KAT

Present Day

I left for class the next morning still with the sense that there were unwanted eyes on me. I jumped when I saw a black town car at the curb, but Bryan's driver was waiting by the door.

"Hi. Mr. Leighton sent me for you."

My reflex was to decline—I didn't want special treatment, or anyone to see me getting special treatment. But I was so relieved to avoid the streets where anyone could follow me, and these were special circumstances. I slid into the back seat only to find I was alone. "Excuse me. Where's Bryan?"

"He asked me to drive you wherever you needed for the next few days."

"Why?"

"He didn't say."

I rooted around in my bag for my phone, texting Bryan again.

Kat: Hey! Is everything OK?

This situation was veering too close to the one with my college ex-boyfriend Michael, and I wasn't someone who craved danger like a drug.

But Bryan didn't respond.

The driver took me to class, and I expected him to drop me off curbside. Instead, he stepped out of the car, scanned the street in each direction, and then placed a hand on my back and led me into the building, as if he were a secret service agent on my security detail.

"Are things worse?"

"Not that I'm aware of. They're meeting with the lawyers and Mr. Wilco today. This is just a precaution Mr. Leighton wanted to take."

That seemed reasonable enough, though still scary.

"I'll be here when class ends," the driver replied, and that was clearly all the information I was getting.

* * *

Sure enough, the driver was waiting inside the lobby of the business building in the early afternoon. I started toward the main door, but he gestured down the hallway, wrapped a hand around my elbow, and guided me to a back door that led to the building's rarely used service exit. There, the car was waiting.

"Okay, now I'm getting nervous with this whole cloak-and-dagger operation." Especially when Bryan hadn't texted me back that morning. "Is Bryan . . . Mr. Leighton . . . okay?"

"I would imagine so," the driver said. *Imagine.* He didn't know. "Where can I take you, Miss Harper?" he asked as he started the car.

I gave him the address of a café where I was meeting Claire, and he drove me there, standing guard outside as Claire and I sipped hot chocolate and I tried to pretend my day hadn't been turned upside down with covert affairs.

"I want a full report when you return from Paris," Claire said. "I'll be out of the country for a week. I convinced my husband to take me away on a technology-free trip to Tahiti."

"A trip without tech. How daring!'"

She whispered clandestinely, "I'm not sure I'll make it without my blogs. But I will do my best."

We chatted about being dependent on our phones, and boy, did I ever feel tethered to mine. It was all I could do not to pick it up every time I took a breath in the conversation. I wanted to hear from Bryan. Wanted to know what was going on.

* * *

When it was time to head home, I settled into the safety of the leather seats of the town car, closed my eyes, and tried desperately to let go of the caged-in day and my worry. Then, as we idled in the stalled Park Avenue traffic, I heard the driver's phone ring. My ears pricked as he answered.

"Hello?"

In his pause, I could make out the gravelly sound of the other voice. Nicole Blazer.

"Yes?"

A pause.

"She's with me right now."

Another pause, and a strange fear ricocheted through my body.

"I'll bring her."

He ended the call and looked at me in the rearview mirror. "Nicole says Bryan has been asking for you."

Nicole placed a gentle hand on my arm. "It's not dire, but his hand is pretty banged up."

"What on earth happened?"

Nicole held open the pristinely painted white door that led into the foyer of Bryan's brownstone on Sixtieth and Park. "We were meeting with Wilco and his attorneys this afternoon to review the wrongful termination suit and attempt to settle. We were all there, and one minute it was tense but civil, and the next it got personal. Bryan kept his cool, but then Wilco sucker-punched him."

My eyes widened with shock. "Oh my God. Really?" I pressed my hand to my mouth, but then lowered it to ask, "Did Bryan hit him back? Is that how he injured his hand?"

Nicole grimaced. "No. He stumbled against the marble-topped table and sprained his hand."

"But he's okay except for that?" I asked. "What happened with Wilco?"

"It all happened so quickly. The security guard at the office rushed in and restrained Wilco, and his attorneys tried to calm everything down, then the police came a few minutes later and arrested him."

"For hitting Bryan?" I tried to wrap my head around the scene.

Nicole nodded. "Partly for that, but mostly because Wilco has been harassing him with late-night phone calls, and then he called *me* last night. That's why Bryan sent his car for you this morning. To keep you safe all day." I didn't realize I was shaking until Nicole put her arms around me. "Hey. You're okay. Everyone's okay. Wilco's in police custody now, and his lawyers told him he'd blown any chance of a wrongful termination suit."

"Where's Bryan? How is he?"

She gestured toward the staircase. "Upstairs on the living room couch. Everybody freaked out, and the board made him go to the hospital to make sure he hadn't broken his hand. They gave him some pain meds." She allowed herself a slight grin. "Apparently, he's a bit of a lightweight where those are concerned. Then he kept asking for you."

I felt some of the fear leave my body. "He did?"

Nicole nodded and led the way upstairs. "He said he wanted to see you. Insisted I call you."

I followed her, unsure of what to expect. When I reached the living room, Bryan was stretched out on the couch, his head resting on a pillow, the TV on a low volume. He was wearing a checkered button-down shirt and dark-gray pants, but his shoes were off, kicked onto the hardwood floor. His sleeves were rolled up and his right hand was bandaged.

When he saw me, he smiled as if I were the answer to any question. "Hey, you."

I melted at the sound of his voice and the warmth in his eyes. His smile was soft and just a little loopy. It was a little bit adorable. I walked over to him.

"Sit down," he said, pointing to the couch.

I walked over and sat gingerly on the edge, not wanting to hurt him. I pointed to the elastic bandage wrapping his hand. "Does it hurt?"

"Not now. Those little white pills have worked their voodoo magic."

I laughed once. "I bet. Are you okay?"

"Yeah. And if I'd known all I had to do to get rid of a lawsuit was let him land a punch, I'd have done it sooner."

"Don't say that."

"Kat, do you want something to drink?" The question came from Nicole.

"I'm okay."

"Bryan? More water?"

"How about a beer? When can I have one of those?

Or maybe we should get champagne to celebrate the suit being dropped."

Nicole rolled her eyes and headed upstairs, leaving us alone.

"So," I began, not sure where I was going.

"So," he replied, and flashed me another one of his woozy smiles.

"Those pain meds must be good."

"Not as good as you." Then he reached his unbandaged hand into my hair and pulled me closer, bringing my lips to his and kissing me softly. It was the last thing I expected, but it was the thing I wanted most in the world. I gave in to the kiss, to the way his lips knew mine, to the way he tasted sweet and salty at the same time. "Now, I feel much better."

He closed his eyes and fell asleep.

* * *

Nicole didn't know everything. But she knew enough.

"It wasn't that hard to figure out," she said as we sat on the metal stools in Bryan's kitchen while he dozed. Nicole's feet dangled, making her look even tinier.

"Really?"

"I noticed how he talked about you. I think you're pretty brilliant too, but there was something else in his voice. Something more vulnerable. And then yesterday in my office when you looked at him as he walked away, it all clicked."

I dropped my head in my hands. "I'm so obvious."

"No. You're just in love." Nicole sounded like a gruff, tough chick doling out truisms with that husky voice of hers.

"But we're not supposed to be," I said.

She waved a hand. "When are we ever supposed to be? I mean, does it ever happen at the right time? I met my partner on a work project too. There are always complications in every relationship."

"Did he say anything?" I was fishing for information, but I didn't care. I wanted to know how all our care and discretion had ended up being useless.

But more than that, I wanted to know what happened now. I wanted us to be something, wanted to move beyond texting and flirting, museum visits and coffee shop stops. More than anything I wanted to be in his life.

"I just asked him point-blank at the hospital if he had a thing for you. He said yes." My heart fluttered, and even with Bryan banged up downstairs, I couldn't help but grin wildly. "And he was all worried about the board and how they'd look at it because of Wilco's affair. And then there's Caldwell, who's Captain Conservative."

"Right, and those are all still true."

"Yes, but you're twenty-three and not an employee." Nicole reached out and took my hand. She looked very pleased with herself, like a good matchmaker pulling off a match. "When I asked him if it was the real thing with you, and he said yes to that as well, I told him I'd talk to the board and to Caldwell in particular. The guy's conservative as hell, but he didn't freak out when I brought my partner to the holiday party last year, so I think I can convince him."

That was all I wanted. To be more than just play-mates. To be the real thing. A rush of happiness warmed me all over.

"What about NYU though? And the mentor program?"

"I told Bryan that as long as he recused himself as your mentor, everything should be fine."

Would it? That would leave me without a mentor for the rest of the term, and if I didn't have a mentor, would I have to retake the class? I needed this course in order to graduate.

Too much relied on my graduation for me to think this would be as easy as Nicole thought.

24
———

BRYAN

Five Years Ago

As Kat went into the campus bookstore, I read the email again. This could set the course for my entire career—or at least with this company.

Looks like there might be an opening soon in our Paris office. You're fluent, right? Let's talk Monday about this.

Equal parts excitement and surprise raced through me. My boss had mentioned working abroad in their Paris branch, but it had never occurred to me that it might happen so quickly. When I'd interviewed for the job, it hadn't occurred to me that there would be someone I cared about leaving behind. Now I realized

I might be separated from Kat by an ocean. I wanted to stay, but I wanted to go.

When I found her in the bookstore, I must have looked as conflicted as I felt, because she asked if everything was okay.

"Yeah, it's great actually," I said, because I *did* want this. I did want the opportunity to learn and grow in my career. I was just starting out and this would broaden the world of possibilities open to me. "I might be going to Paris soon. To work."

"That's amazing!" She laughed and threw her arms around me.

"You'll have to come visit me," I said. I wanted to see how she'd respond. Was it even fair of me to suggest it, visiting a guy she'd known less than three months? Coming down to New York was one thing, and she would be living here soon.

She pulled back to look at me, a wide smile on her gorgeous face. "You know I'd be there in a heartbeat to see you."

And that's the moment. Right there. When every-thing became all too clear. A little moment. A sweet comment. Everything that should melt my heart. And it did. That was the trouble. I loved her too much to let her miss what might be the best part of her life... for me.

How weird that her agreement, her excitement, would bring everything to a screeching halt. Was I really going to ask her to fly across the ocean when she should be enjoying college, her first time living away from home? I wouldn't trade my college years for anything—I'd learned as much about myself as I had in class. What if being with me kept her from discovering all that she could?

We were both starting out, in different ways. I'd have to discover who I was as a businessman. Could I do that and give Kat all the attention and support she deserved? Especially if I was on another continent.

Staying together wasn't going to work. It wasn't fair to her. Keeping her in my life would only enhance it, but I didn't think I could say the opposite was true. I had to step back. That's what my conscience told me. I didn't want to hold her back from anything, and I knew staying together would *only* do that. I wanted her to be free to live her life fully in college, without the burden of a boyfriend across an ocean.

I kissed her hard that night when I put her on the train back to Mystic, wishing it didn't feel like it might be the last time.

25

KAT

Present Day

Nicole headed for her own home, leaving me with a pint of Ben & Jerry's Chocolate Therapy. All I could think was how Bryan might be free and clear, but there was no way I would come out of this unscathed. Not right now, at least. Any possibility of an *us* would have to go back on hold once again. I couldn't have him end the mentorship. I needed to finish school for a million reasons.

I went to the kitchen, feeling a bit like an intruder as I rooted around for two spoons. I'd never been in his place before, and now here I was, for all intents and purposes taking care of him after a trip to the ER.

I found a white wood-paneled drawer that held utensils, grabbed two spoons, snagged two cloth napkins from the holder on the island, and returned to the living room. Bryan was awake now, reading a book on his tablet. Night had fallen, and the lights were dimmed. There was just enough illumination that I could look over the room again.

The hardwood floors were a polished blond, and the walls were eggshell colored, giving the room warmth. There were a few pieces of art on the walls— reproductions of the Magritte with an apple in front of a man's face and of Mark Rothko's abstract images in solid red. The couch was comfortable and classy in a dove-gray color, and the coffee table was made of a sheet of sturdy glass atop two brushed metal blocks.

When he saw me, he set his tablet aside. I joined him on the couch, opened the pint of ice cream, and presented him with a spoon.

"My favorite. How did you know?"

"Nicole knew, silly."

"It was a rhetorical question," he said with a lopsided smile.

He dug into the ice cream, and I joined him. We ate quietly for a minute, but after a few bites, he put the spoon down on the coffee table. I placed my spoon and the pint next to it. "Did Nicole tell you?" he asked.

"Tell me what?"

"Anything interesting?" he asked with a side-eye, watching for my reaction.

"She told me about the mediation, and how that all went down."

He leaned back on the couch cushion and looked up at the ceiling. "You think you know a guy . . ." Then he picked his head back up and looked at me. "You don't have to worry about being followed anymore. That was Wilco's private investigator. Now that the suit's settled, he is off the job."

"Wilco sicced a private investigator on me?" We hadn't given him anything to see, but the idea of being spied on made me shudder.

"Well, on me, but then on you too. He wanted something to show my 'hypocrisy' to the board. Nice, huh? I can't forgive him for putting you through that."

"You too. Not just me."

He shifted so he could face me and cupped my face with his hand. Not just a brush, but a proper touch. "I know you have a lot riding on this class. I couldn't forgive myself if being with me ruined that for you."

He was clear and direct, and my heart was about to burst. "But now that's over."

"Yes."

"No more PI."

"Nope." His hand curled around the back of my head. "Just you and me."

I was a flood of colors. I was the center of a sunburst as my heart beat faster, and happiness rushed all through the freeways of the intersecting veins inside my body, filling me with everything good in the world.

I put all that feeling into kissing him, closing the gap between us and giving in entirely. He pulled me to him, kissing me deeper, closer. My arms wrapped around his neck while my hands worked their way up into his soft hair. His good hand pressed firmly into my back, while his bandaged one rested by his side.

My hunger for him was deeper than that afternoon at the factory, and here we were, Bryan's lips on mine, sweeter than the ice cream that would be a chocolate puddle if we kept going like this.

But we couldn't keep going like this. We had to figure out what *this* was.

I pulled back. "We need to talk."

He tensed, but then shifted to a sitting position and to his standard business voice. "Okay."

I was reminded how quickly he could segue from one mode to another. I wasn't sure if that was an admirable trait or not.

"Nicole told me the advice she gave you. That we could pursue a relationship or whatever." I found myself blushing and looked away when I said the words.

He smirked, but it turned into a grin. "'A relationship or whatever'? Is that what the kids are calling it? Relationships or whatever?"

I pretended to punch his arm.

"Hey. I'm damaged goods now. Be careful."

"Anyway. So, yeah. Relationship or whatever."

"Do we call it boyfriend-girlfriend? Or is that too high school? Lovers just seems so weird. Especially since, you know, I haven't seen you fully naked yet."

"Okay. I thought we were being serious," I said, but it occurred to me that maybe he was avoiding the serious conversation.

"Fine. I'm serious."

"We can't be involved until I graduate. Professor Oliver won't stand for it. And I have to get my degree.

Not just to get the investment in my business, but because I want to. We have to really, truly, for real this time put everything on hold. Yes, we could sneak around. Yes, we could try not to get caught. But I want to do things the right way. I want to start over with you in the open, not in hiding."

I squared my shoulders. I couldn't yield to wishes, or him, or my feelings. "I guess what I'm saying is you have to be my mentor. You can't recuse yourself, or I might not be able to finish school."

He raised an eyebrow. "Oh, you're kind of giving me an order."

"Kind of. Or more like a request. Stay my mentor for the next few weeks, and then when I graduate, we can . . ."

"Be together?"

"Yes. But we really have to cool it till then. No taking chances. No calls. No nothing."

"I think I could be amenable to waiting for you—under one condition."

"What's that?"

He put his good hand on my waist and gently pulled my chest to his. Then he whispered in my ear, his voice low and smoky, "Stay with me a little while tonight. Just to hold me—us—over until then."

"That . . . seems fair."

"Fair enough." He reached for me with his left hand, shifting my body alongside his and spooning me on the couch. He layered kisses on the back of my neck that turned me inside out. He pushed my hair out of the way and traced his tongue lazily across my skin, over my earlobe, and down to my shoulder blade. He moved his hand to my waist, slipping his fingers underneath my sweater. I gave in to the feeling of his fingers dancing on the waistband of my jeans. His hand was warm, his skin was soft, he felt amazing. I closed my eyes.

"Good thing I'm left-handed," he said.

Even though I could feel the soft little hairs on my arms standing on end, I moved his hand off my belly. "Yes. That means you can use your left hand to work the TV remote."

He heaved a long, laborious sigh of playful resignation.

"You have a will of steel, and it only makes me want to get you naked even more. But for now, I surrender. Want to watch a movie?"

"I'd love nothing more."

I handed him the remote and settled in next to him. We scrolled through the options on demand, debating whether we wanted to see *Pitch Perfect* or *Bridesmaids*. Anna Kendrick was my girl crush, so her movie won. Plus, I didn't have to worry about whether that sexy scene where the cop and Kristen Wiig spend the night together would make me break my vow.

Besides, it was better this way, curled up and warm in his arms. For tonight at least.

26

Bryan: I woke up next to an empty Ben & Jerry's pint.

Kat: Was it good?

Bryan: You tell me. I can't remember devouring it. Did you?

Kat: Nice try. But nope. I am not to blame for the empty carton. My best guess? You finished it for breakfast this morning.

Bryan: Ah! I had it on French toast.

Kat: Has anyone told you your sweet tooth is the size of Texas?

Bryan: Yes. You.

Bryan: Also, thank you.

Kat: I didn't get the ice cream.

Bryan: No, Kat. Thank you for coming to see me. For being there. For listening. Thank you for all the times we've talked over the last few months.

Kat: Are you still on pain meds?

Bryan: No. This is all me. From the heart. You're amazing.

Kat: So are you. And I've loved all our talks too.

Bryan: Same. I've loved all this time with you. Also, your lips are spectacular.

Bryan: I didn't dream that last night, did I?

Kat: If you did, we had the same one. That's how I know yours are spectacular too.

Bryan: Good. It's okay if I forgot I ate the ice cream, but I would never, ever want to forget kissing you.

27

KAT

Present Day

I surveyed my open suitcase, thumbing through my folded clothes and neatly aligned shoes. I was ready for four days in Paris. As I double-checked that I'd packed a power adaptor, and triple-checked that I'd included extra tights—November is cold in the City of Lights—I chewed the inside of my cheek with worry.

What if I returned from Paris empty-handed? Or worse, what if I brought back a brilliant prototype for a new line of necklaces and it still wasn't what Claire and her contacts at the Elizabeth's department store had in mind? Where would my parents be then? I had a chance with Claire; it was in my grasp, and I needed to hold on tight and not let go.

I took a deep breath and shut my black suitcase. Then I checked my computer bag, made sure my passport was secure, and finally looked up the weather on my phone. A storm was headed toward Manhattan in a day or so. I would probably escape the city in the nick of time.

I'd just moved the suitcase and flopped onto my bed with my e-reader when I heard the front door crash wide open. Jill always had to make an entrance.

"Kat! I have to tell you my news!"

Her heels banged across the floor as she ran down the hall and jumped onto my bed.

"Tell me your news before you explode."

"I got a callback for the new musical. The new Frederick Stillman musical," she said. "He is a *legend*. Actors will do *anything* to be in his shows, and *I* have a callback!"

I knocked fists with her. "You are a rock star!"

She twisted her index and middle finger together. "Don't jinx me. But I hope so! I hope I'm a Broadway star." She flopped back on my bed. "Oh my God, Kat. This is my dream. A role in a Stillman musical. It's called *Crash the Moon*, and the score is to die for. Well, the song they gave me. It's a rock ballad I have to sing. But the casting director saw my Eponine and called me in for a supporting role. And the director is none other than the Tony-winning Davis Milo."

"I didn't even know you were auditioning for it."

"I didn't tell a soul. I was terrified I'd blow it, so I kept it totally secret. Now they want to bring me in for the producer next week. It's a good thing you'll be gone because I'll pretty much just be practicing my song whenever I'm not coaching my newest half-marathon club."

"You're going to blow them away and make gobs of money as a star. Break a leg."

My phone rang. Jill raised an eyebrow as she picked it up from my nightstand and brandished it at me. "If it isn't Mr. Hottie McCuff Links. I thought you two were cooling it until after the semester was over."

I sat up straight and looked at Bryan's name on the screen. I wanted to hear his voice. I also wanted to be strong. Jill decided the matter when she swiped her finger over the phone.

"Kat in the Box's line. How may I help you?"

I rolled my eyes as she waited.

"No, I don't believe she is available. She'll be free again to speak with you in about five weeks." Jill spoke in a professional voice as if she were my receptionist.

A pause. Jill smirked and nodded several times. "My, my, my. Isn't that just convenient that the padlock deal came through."

My shoulders tightened with excitement. Padlocks. That could only mean one thing.

"Oh, really? Well, you definitely shouldn't go anywhere near the Hotel Le Marquis that's just three blocks from the Eiffel Tower on rue Dupleix when you go to Paris tomorrow." Jill clasped her hand over her mouth in an overly dramatic gesture. "Oh my. I did not mean to drop the name of Kat's hotel. Especially since you two have your chastity belts on. Pretend I didn't mention it. Wipe it from your brain.

I'll make sure she knows to stay away from the W Hotel too. Ta-ta for now."

She hung up the phone, and I stared at her, mouth agape.

She shrugged. "What was I to do? He was giving you a heads-up that the city of Paris called him in for some last-minute meeting about the padlocks, whatever that means. He didn't want you to be surprised if you see him at the airport tomorrow. He said he had to move up his flight a day because of the storm." Jill winked. "Convenient, that Mother Nature, isn't she?"

Très convenient. Or inconvenient. Depending on how you looked at it.

28

KAT

Five Years Ago

The only thing better than strolling around my new campus was strolling around it with Bryan. In July, not every building was open, but there were enough people on campus to help me imagine what it would be like.

"I can't believe I'm going to be here in a month! It's going to be amazing." I squeezed Bryan's hand as we walked along the outside of one of the dorms. "Did you love it here?"

"Yes. I loved it," he said, seeming nostalgic. "And you'll have a ton of fun too."

"I can't wait to start. I know I'm going to love it."

"You are," Bryan said, but there was something sad in his tone.

I looked at him. "Hey. You okay?"

"Totally."

"Because you sounded . . ."

"I'm fine."

We checked out the café where I could see myself doing all my homework, and the library, which was speckled with students for the summer session. But since we'd left the campus bookstore, Bryan's mind seemed elsewhere, and he didn't tell me where he'd gone.

At the station on Sunday night, waiting for the last train to Mystic, I thanked him again for the necklace.

"You should always wear it." He sounded so wistful, and when he kissed me goodbye, the moment turned melancholy. I didn't feel like a girl who was returning in a week. I felt like a girl being sent off with only an Eiffel Tower necklace to remember him by.

I told myself I was worrying for nothing. That he was probably already thinking about the work week ahead. But when I called a few days later to confirm our weekend plans, I knew I wasn't imagining things. His voice was different. Strained and distant.

"I don't think you should come in," he said.

We'd been planning this weekend for more than a month. My unsettled feeling had become worry, which climbed toward panic. "Why? Did something come up at work?"

"No. It's just . . . I don't think we should . . ."

"Don't think we should what?"

There were many ways to answer the question, but the scariest one was what he said next.

"I don't think we should be together."

I looked at my phone as if it were a radio tuned to a station in another language. Then I raised it back to my ear and said the only thing I could think of. The thing I was clinging to. "But I'm totally in love with you, Bryan. One hundred percent and then some. And I want to be with you."

Then I waited. And I waited. And I waited.

Words didn't come. Not *those* words and not any others.

The silence choked me, gripping me around the neck.

How could I have misread him so badly? He'd said he was falling for me. Where else do you fall but in love?

Then he spoke, and his words were sharp glass. "It's the same for me. But we can't be together. I have to go."

The screen told me the call had ended, but not why. I ripped off the necklace Bryan had given me, breaking the clasp in a single fierce pull, then I tossed it into the trash, stuffing it at the bottom of the can.

I could hear his words the rest of the day, and on through the night—the pause before he spoke, the shape of each and every syllable. The words *it's the same for me* were meaningless when followed by *but we can't be together. I have to go.*

That's exactly what he did. He left.

29

KAT

Present Day

The lights of the city shone like fireflies as New York City fell away below me. The plane soared higher, and I worked on a crossword puzzle, filling in "edict" as the answer for a five-letter word for "doctrine." How apropos, given my self-imposed edict to stay away from Bryan for the next five weeks. I didn't see him when I boarded, but I suspected he was in first class, and I was stuck in lowly coach.

As I finished the puzzle, one of my least favorite odors permeated the air—the scent of smelly man-foot. The guy next to me had removed his shoes. I wrinkled my nose and tried to breathe through my mouth.

"Ah, that's better," he said to the woman with him as he wiggled his freed feet in their white tube socks.

The woman smiled without showing any teeth, and then began clipping her nails.

Great. Now I had not one, but two things from my never-do-in-public list right in my row. At least I had the aisle seat. I turned, shifting my body away from them and hoping the lady might gently remind her man of proper social mores.

But after several minutes of sweaty-sock-scented air and the clip-clip-clip of nail maintenance, I started to wonder if perhaps my seatmates might break out Q-tips next and check for earwax. I frowned at the image as the plane reached its cruising altitude, and one of the flight attendants strolled down the aisle, a purposeful look in her eyes. When she reached me, she bent down. She wore her hair in a perfectly coiffed twist.

"*Bon soir.* You are Ms. Harper?"

"*Bon soir.* I am."

"If you'd like, I can move you to a row closer up."

"You can?"

"Yes, the seats are much more comfortable, and there is a spare one."

She didn't have to ask twice. I grabbed my computer bag, unbuckled, and followed the sharp-suited woman. She escorted me out of coach, held open the blue curtain to economy plus, and guided me through the cushier section. I spotted a few empty seats, but she didn't stop. She marched forward to the next blue curtain, the one that led to first class. I slowed my pace when I realized where she was taking me. The empty seat was next to Bryan. He turned around, smiled with his eyes, and gestured grandly to the massive leather seat next to his, so large it could turn into a bed. He no longer had a bandage on his right hand.

"Would you care to join me? The seat is empty, and I have plenty of miles, so it's not a problem."

"Yes, yes, yes. The guy next to me had his shoes off and his wife was cutting her nails."

"Those activities are forbidden under my regime."

"I know!"

I took the seat, buckled in, and leaned against the buttery leather chair, feeling like a princess flying through the sky to Paris.

"Would you like to see the wine list?"

A dark-skinned woman with light-brown eyes proffered what looked like an invitation to a fancy party. I tried not to let my jaw drop. They weren't just passing out diet sodas and seltzer here in first class. There were several varieties of wine on the list, not to mention cocktails. I looked at Bryan. "Are you getting something?"

"I'm not really a wine person. I'll take a Glenlivet on the rocks," he said to the flight attendant. Then to me, "You?"

I shook my head.

"Would you like a cocktail, then?"

"Just an orange juice, please." I felt like a kid, but the truth was, I didn't trust myself not to pounce on

Bryan if I had a drink or two in me. She nodded and walked away.

"Not in the mood? Or do you really not drink?"

"Not often."

"What's that all about? Any reason?"

"No. No deep-seated childhood trauma. No dysfunction I'm trying to avoid. The truth is I just don't like the taste of alcohol."

"Not even champagne or cosmopolitans or chocolate martinis? With your sweet tooth, I would think you'd be all over the chocolate martinis."

"Ugh. No. None of them. Those fruity drinks and sweet drinks—all they're doing is trying to add enough sweet stuff to mask the taste of the liquor. And I can't stand the taste of beer. I mean, I drank it in college. But now it just reminds me that I never really liked the taste even then. It's like swill."

"And hard liquors are out, I assume?"

"They taste like gasoline to me. Well, I've never had gasoline, of course. My mother would correct me now and say, 'You mean they taste like gasoline smells.'"

The flight attendant reappeared with our drinks. She placed Bryan's sturdy glass of scotch on his tray table alongside my orange juice and two glasses of water. After she left, Bryan held up his glass to toast.

"I'm glad to see your hand is better."

"Just a sprain. It's pretty much back to normal now."

"Good."

"To a successful business trip to Paris." We clinked glasses.

"I will definitely drink to that." I took a sip of my orange juice. "So, how did it all come together? The padlock thing?"

"It's not a done deal. But I've been waiting on the city, and I heard this week that there's someone new in charge, and she wants to meet right away."

"How exciting! You've been wanting this for some time."

"I think it's going to be a great way to make something out of a symbol that lots of people love," he said.

"Here's a question for you. If you hadn't started this company, if you were doing something else entirely, what would it be?"

"You mean, like playing shortstop for the New York Yankees?"

"Yes. Like that."

"Well, shortstop for sure. Otherwise, I'd have to say rock star."

"Rock star would be awesome."

"And after that, I'd say write for a wine magazine."

I chuckled. "A wine magazine? I thought you didn't like wine."

"I don't like wine. When you write for a wine magazine, you can say anything you want, and no one will challenge you."

"Explain."

"You just make it up. You ever read that stuff?"

"Well, no. Obviously."

"Oh, I do. Just for fun." He launched into an imitation of a wine writer, pretending to hold a glass and swirl it with one hand, while taking notes with the other. "Mmm, I taste a little sandpaper. Yes, sandpaper and fresh soil."

He sniffed an imaginary glass. "Faint aromas of shoe leather mixed with lightly toasted tar. It's full-bodied, velvety, and long. With just a touch of gravel." He scoffed. "Gravel. I mean, it's like you said with gasoline—how many people know what gravel tastes like? But people take that seriously."

I gestured to my glass. "Well, my orange juice tastes like it came from the sunshine-kissed regions of Florida, with just a hint of tropical flavor and an extra dash of pulp."

Bryan raised his hands, palms out. "See? Nothing to it. But you know what I'd really like to write about in a wine magazine?"

"What would you like to write about?" I took another drink of my juice.

"I'd say, I like going to Bob's Java Hut down by the ballpark and getting an egg salad sandwich before a Yankees game. That and a two-dollar Bud. And I don't even like Bud. But it's good before a baseball game."

I laughed again, but I'd just taken a drink of my non-drink.

"The complexity of the egg salad sandwich, the mayonnaise from the grocery store, the smoky balance between the mayonnaise and the eggs . . ."

I couldn't swallow my drink while I was laughing, but I couldn't stop.

"Sometimes I can even taste the shell from the egg.

I can almost smell the chicken from where they failed to clean the egg."

I covered my mouth, trying hard not to spit out the liquid, my eyes tearing up.

"Oh, shit. I'm sorry, Kat." Bryan handed me a glass of water. I shook my head. If I couldn't swallow the juice, what was I supposed to do with that? There were only two ways out—mouth or nose.

OJ is hell on the sinuses. I reached for a napkin to cover my face, mortified as the juice made its way out my nostrils and into the napkin. Hiding as best I could, I dropped my face onto the table.

"Are you okay, Kat?" He placed a hand on my arm.

I spoke, voice muffled by the napkin. "You can't take me anywhere. You might as well send me back to coach."

"I could never banish you to the land of smelly feet. I'm keeping you up here." Bryan gently petted my hair. Even the soothing touch of his hand after my display of dorkitude felt good. "Besides, it was all my fault."

I sat up straight. "You're right. It is all your fault. You made me laugh. You totally did it on purpose. You sit there and launch into one of your riffs, and you make me snort juice."

"They say laughter is the way to a woman's heart."

I lowered my voice. "You already have my heart. Or you will after the semester is over."

His smile was warm. "I'll just stake my claim on it, then."

My heart felt warm too, and I let it out through my

smile. "You've always made me laugh. You've always made me happy."

Bryan looked out the window for a moment, at the dark of night rushing past the plane. He turned back to me. The look in his green eyes was intense and unreadable.

"What is it?"

"There's something I've always wanted to tell you."

I was wary of how sober he'd gotten. "That doesn't sound like a good something."

"It's not bad, I swear." He placed his hands on his thighs. He parted his lips but didn't speak right away. I watched him as he fumbled for words, watched his throat as he swallowed. He closed his eyes briefly, then opened them to hold my gaze, a tight, sharp line between us. I felt as if I were hanging on to something that could crash in an instant. "Do you remember when you told me you loved me the first time?"

How could anyone forget her first love not loving her back? The memory was always in reach.

"Yes."

"And I said, 'It's the same for me. But we can't be together. I have to go'?"

My face tightened, and I stared hard at the seat in front of me. "Do we need to reenact it?"

"No. Because I handled it terribly."

I turned back to stare at him as if he'd just spoken Russian. "What?"

"I meant it when I said it's the same for me. But I should have told you directly. Because I was crazy in love with you then. Just like I am now. I've always loved you. I never stopped."

My head was spinning. My heart sputtered. I felt as if the plane had disappeared and I was flailing in the cold, dark atmosphere, not knowing which way I was tumbling.

"Why did you say we can't be together then?"

"Because after we walked around NYU together, all I could think was that I would be holding you back. That's why I was quiet that day. I just kept thinking it would be wrong. That it would be unfair to you if you went to college and were already saddled with an older boyfriend. I didn't want to be the guy who dragged you down. I wanted you to go to be away from home, meet other guys, figure out what you wanted in life. I wanted you to experience life on your own terms. And I knew I was going to be leaving the country, and it seemed too unfair to you to ask you to wait for me or to be a long-distance girlfriend."

I scoffed. "Instead, you broke my heart."

He reached for my hand and traced a line across my palm. His touch was so soft, but I still felt raw and exposed. "Forgive me," he said.

I didn't respond. Instead, I looked deeply into his eyes, pools of green I could lose myself in. How I'd loved getting lost in him and being found by him again. He leaned closer, pressed his forehead against mine, and took my hands in his.

"Forgive me for lying. Forgive me for breaking your heart," he whispered to me, his voice soft and fragile and tender.

This was what I'd always longed to hear. That he'd loved me the way I'd loved him. Not "it's the same for me." But I found it only reopened the wound, in a fresh way. He'd thought he knew what was best for me. But he was wrong. And if he'd thought that feeling so damn unwanted by my first love would be good for me, had he really known me at all?

I pulled away from him. "I wish you had told me that back then. I wish you had let us make that decision together. Instead, you made me think you didn't love me, and it hurt so fucking much."

"I'm sorry, Kat. I'm truly, truly sorry."

He looked so anguished. But that didn't make my heart hurt any less. It didn't change the past, and it didn't fix the present.

"Hey, do you want to watch a movie?" he asked, worry lining his voice. He tipped his forehead to the screen on the back of the seats. "I think I saw *Love Actually* on the list for this flight."

One of my all-time favorites.

But I couldn't. I couldn't just go back in time with him as if that would take the pain away.

"I think I'm going to read," I said, then turned away and buried myself in a book for the rest of the flight.

30

KAT

Present Day

In the morning, I met my friend Elise at a café on a cobbled street corner near her home in Montmartre. She smiled widely and stood when she saw me, kissing me on each cheek as the French do. She was French-American and had been living there for several years, running her own ad agency. I emailed her when I knew I'd be taking this trip—I hadn't seen her since I was last here, and I was looking forward to catching up now.

"You look stunning," she told me.

"As do you," I said. She was a petite brunette in cat's-eye glasses, adorable but sexy too.

"How long will you be in town? Whatever the answer is, it's not long enough."

I told her just a few days, then we ordered breakfast. Over eggs and baguettes, she shared her latest news, then mentioned a man she'd been seeing.

My eyebrows rose. Her last relationship ended in one of the worst ways possible, so I was thrilled to hear she'd found a new one that was making her happier.

"His name is Christian. He's British, charming, brilliant, and he makes me laugh and swoon," she said with a grin. "As you can imagine, I have no clue if I should run for the hills or run to him."

I laughed. "I can understand the dilemma. Once you find a good one, it can be terrifying to move forward, only because you know what the other side of heartbreak is."

She nodded sagely. "I know it far too well." She sighed, but then smiled again. "Enough about me. Tell me more about you."

I gave her a brief overview of Bryan, and we concluded that navigating relationships was often harder than learning a new language.

Then I said goodbye and headed on my first expedition.

* * *

The last time I went to the markets of Paris, I strolled indulgently through the wares, lingering over anything that caught my fancy.

This time I was efficiency personified as I tackled Porte de Vanves a few days later, powering through table after table, row after row. I scanned quickly, writing off the items I obviously would never use on a necklace—candlesticks, picture frames, goblets.

I ignored the old clothes for sale, the chipped sets of china, and the antique mirrors. I stopped at a table with miniature figurines—tiny cows and pigs and dogs and cats no bigger than thimbles. Some were brushed silver, some white porcelain. They were cute, and while I wasn't too sure a cow was anyone's favorite, there was something about the dogs and cats that spoke to me.

I asked the vendor how much. A round woman in a heavy tarp of a dress barked out a number.

"Too high," I answered in French.

We bargained like that until she reached her rock bottom, and I scooped up nearly one hundred cats and dogs, tucking them in my wheeled shopping bag. I felt like a regular Frenchwoman, weaving in and out of the stalls, wheeling and dealing, snagging the best prices.

I continued on, passing strange-looking garden tools and old kitchen utensils, when I spied several tables full of brooches and pins. They were tiny things and would look so very French on a necklace, the perfect mix of new and vintage. I bought a few dozen and then moved along to another aisle.

I walked past a table full of gray-haired men playing cards as they sucked on cigarettes. They were seated behind a counter displaying a messy array of hammers. I laughed silently, picturing a big, rusty hammer hanging from a slender silver chain. Yeah, that'd be a big hit for sure. I looked beyond the counter and spied a huge box full of antique skeleton keys. The box was at the foot of the card table where the men sat, and it held hundreds upon hundreds of keys that must have worked in miniature locks, because they were no bigger than thumbnails. They weren't rusted, but just the right amount of weathered.

I asked the men how much.

"For the keys?"

"Yes."

A man laughed, showing crooked, yellowed teeth. He took a drag of his cigarette, inhaling deeply. "No one's ever asked before. You want to take them off our hands?"

"Maybe."

"Five euros."

I pursed my lips and resisted breaking out in a smile. The keys were perfect. They were pretty, but they also said something. Keys were staples of charm necklaces, with a universal appeal, but these particular keys had a unique look that stood out, a sense that they could unlock stories, or hearts, or secrets.

"Sold."

I handed the man a bill; he stuffed it in his pocket and gave me the battered cardboard box. I closed the top and managed to stuff the whole thing inside my cavernous shopping bag. I wheeled it away, made a few more stops, then hailed a taxi. As we raced toward the Eiffel Tower, passing cafés full of people lingering over salads and breads and coffees, and bakeries peddling croissants and *tarte*

Normande and chocolate eclairs, I replayed my three days in Paris.

At a market in the Marais, I'd found boxes of star, sun, and moon trinkets. At a street vendor in Montmartre, I'd stumbled across elegant glass hearts. I'd still have to do the hard work of assembling the necklaces, but I had the materials, and they looked both fresh and French.

In the evenings, I'd taken myself out to dinner, at a bistro near Notre-Dame, at a café tucked at the end of a courtyard, and at a bustling Korean place around the corner from the hotel. I'd been alone, but Paris has a way of surrounding people and making sure they don't feel quite so lonely. I'd also stayed far away from the W Hotel near the Opera House—and from Bryan. The fact that I hadn't set up my cell phone for international calling helped. No one could reach me easily.

The taxi driver stopped at the light at one of the boulevards, and I admired the buildings. They had that elegant, centuries-old look about them, with long, tall, open windows. When the light changed, the driver zipped across traffic, took a sharp turn, and let me out at my hotel.

As I pressed the button for the elevator, the desk clerk called out to me.

"Ms. Harper. There is a message here for you."

"For me?"

Perhaps it was Mrs. Oliver, but she was on her vacation. I hoped something hadn't happened to my parents. The clerk handed me a small white envelope.

It was sealed, but my name was on the front. I opened it and unfolded a sheet of paper.

Kat—Remember when you said if I ever needed your translation services that I'd know where to find you? I do need help. Is there any way you can come to dinner tonight? The woman in charge of the padlocks in storage has a My Favorite Mistakes necklace. She loves your designs and would love to meet you. I think it could seal the deal. I hope you'll say yes to dinner at eight. I can send a car for you.

Bryan

There was a phone number for his hotel. I stared at the note as if it would reveal the answer. Should I go? I still felt raw inside now that I knew the truth. I'd been tricked, and even if he'd felt he had to set me free in college, I'd rather he'd have told me he loved me before he left. Instead, he said nothing, and I felt like I was played for a fool.

I was left empty-handed, a broken-hearted idiot.

But if my presence would help Made Here launch a new line of cuff links fashioned out of the leftover promises from the lover's bridge, well, that seemed fitting for our relationship of leftover promises. And it *was* the sort of thing a protégé should do. It was business after all.

I handed the paper to the clerk and asked him to call The W and confirm a car for pickup.

* * *

Orange flames glowed in the nearby fireplace, warming the restaurant. The waiter cleared away our dinner plates as Gabrielle Roussillon informed him that the meal was marvelous. She'd had rabbit and asparagus. I'd had chicken and roasted potatoes, and while I couldn't vouch for the bunny, my French yardbird was indeed fantastic. The white tablecloth was now marked with a splotch of red wine from where Gabrielle had spilled some of her drink while talking with her hands.

Gabrielle was a chatty woman and had commanded the conversation. The pleasant result was I could focus on her rather than Bryan as she told bawdy tales of when she'd lived in Rome, and of all her affairs with Italian men. I laughed, not simply to humor her, but because she was one of those in-your-face people who could tell a saucy tale with a particular panache. She was curvy and broad-shouldered, with sheets of jet-black hair. She wore a ring on her left index finger and mentioned a husband once or twice. I wondered if it was an open marriage. Whether he had a mistress and she had misters, like her Italian lovers. From the conversation, it didn't seem that long ago that she'd been in Italy.

She leaned back in her chair and tapped a charm on her necklace. It was one of mine, and the charm was a pizza pie. "I don't know if you remember this, but I ordered it online from you a year ago."

I flipped through my mental file of necklace

orders. I certainly didn't remember all of them, but a pizza charm stood out. "It's not often that I get a request for a pizza pie. I think I found it at a toy shop. I can't believe that's yours."

"Small world. It's for all my Italian men."

"But of course," Bryan said. I didn't look at him. I'd barely looked at him most of the night. My heart was still sore.

"And yours?" Gabrielle pointed at my throat. "What's on yours?"

I walked her through some of my charms, telling her the same stories I'd told Bryan that afternoon in Washington Square Park—the English major I never became, and the building that I almost moved into.

"And this one?" Gabrielle touched my movie camera charm. "Were you almost a movie director?"

I laughed and shook my head. "No."

"Then what is this for? Is it to remind you to stop watching movies?"

"Sort of." I looked at the fireplace to avoid eye contact. I'd never told Bryan about the movie camera. I'd never told anyone but Jill what it stood for.

"Kat, Kat, Kat. A woman like me knows when a woman is lying. What is the movie camera for?"

I returned my focus to the French civil servant Bryan needed to charm. "It's for a boy."

"And who is this boy?"

"My first love. He was my first favorite mistake."

"Ah. See! I knew it wasn't just about the cinema. Tell me about him." Gabrielle placed her elbow on the table and tucked her chin in her hand, waiting for a story. I glanced briefly at Bryan. He was watching the two of us.

"I met him when I was eighteen."

"Young love. The best kind."

"And he was wonderful. And kind. And funny. He made me laugh. And he kissed like a dream."

"He definitely wasn't a Frenchman, because they kiss like bores!"

"We used to go to the movies together all the time, and we made out in the theater."

"That is why I say young love is the best kind. You can't keep your hands off each other."

I nodded as waiters circled the small restaurant, clearing tables and serving other diners. Low music played overhead, tunes like those sung by the torch singer who'd lived across from me when I'd called this city home. Songs of love gone away or love gone awry.

"But he broke my heart."

"And you vowed to guard your heart?"

"Yes."

"And you still pine for this man?"

"Yes," I said, a hitch in my throat.

"You are beautiful, and you are still so young. We cannot have a young, beautiful, smart woman in love with a boy who doesn't care for her."

"He does care for her." The words came from Bryan. I turned to him, to look into his green eyes with their hints of gold. Those eyes practically infiltrated me with the way they knew me. "He always cared for her. He always loved her. He's madly in love with her. She's his *Love Actually*. She's his *Casablanca*. She's the one he'd stop the bus for, the one he'd dodge traffic for, the one worth sprinting through the terminal to stop the plane. Her name's above the title for him. She's the opening credit and the closing credit. She's the love of his life."

Then, in a voice so low only I could hear, he whispered, "Forgive me."

Hidden by the white tablecloth, I reached for his hand. He laced his fingers through mine, squeezing tight. I squeezed back, and I let go of the hurt. I let go of the ache. I let go of the past.

"He is not a mistake, then," Gabrielle announced.

"He's not. He's the one," I said.

Gabrielle raised her wineglass, now nearly drained of its contents. "We shall drink a toast to love, and drink a toast to business. You have a deal to buy the old padlocks from the city of Paris."

31

KAT

Present Day

Bryan opened the door to the town car he'd reserved. Gabrielle gave him a kiss on each cheek then got inside. He shut the door, and we both waved as the driver sped off to take her home. We crossed the cobbled street and turned onto the sidewalk running along the Seine. The muted yellow gaslight from the street lamps flickered and illuminated our path along the slate-gray ribbon that sliced its way through the city.

"You were amazing back there," he said.

"Oh, you're too sweet."

"I would call you a good luck charm, but I'm pretty sure it's a hell of a lot more than luck that just went down in there." He walked a few steps, glancing at me with a smile in his eyes. "Brains, talent, beauty, brilliance. Is there anything you can't do?"

"I'm not terribly good at cooking or gardening."

He snapped his fingers as if disappointed. Then he turned serious, more earnest. "Kat, thank you. Thank you so much for what you did."

"I'm glad I could be of help."

Bryan reached for my hand. "Am I allowed to hold your hand? Or does that break the on-ice rules?"

"I'll bend on this one, just for a moment."

We turned onto the Pont du Carrousel that arced over the river. A dinner boat tour floated underneath the bridge, its lights drawing yellow squiggly lines along the water. The Louvre watched over us from nearby.

He drew me to a stop and then took my other hand, holding both as we faced each other. Holding my gaze, too, so I couldn't look away. "Would you bend on another one? Because I'd really like to kiss you by the Seine."

I gave barely a nod before he pulled me close and dusted his lips against mine, leaving a soft, wet kiss behind.

"We should stop. We should be good."

"Maybe. But not before I tell you that I'm crazy in love with you, Kat. Before I promise I'll never stop telling you that." He smiled both tenderly and tentatively. "I have five years' worth of I love yous bottled up, and I don't want to hoard them, so I'll say it again. I'm madly in love with you, Kat Harper."

I felt like I was spinning and glimmering, his words lighting a fuse in me. "Fine," I said with a smile, much calmer than I felt. "That earns you one more kiss."

He pressed his lips to mine, tracing them with his tongue and making me shiver. I looped my arms around him, underneath his jacket and against his shirt. He ran his hands through my hair, moving closer. The railing of the bridge was against my back, and the space between us was compressed. My body melted into his, and I inhaled his cool, clean skin. I wanted to feel him, touch him, taste him, have him. I was foolish to ever think I could have resisted.

Maybe I was selfish. Maybe I was stupid. Maybe I could have waited five more weeks.

All of that and more was true.

But I ceased caring and stopped reasoning. I tossed the rules, along with caution, into the Seine.

Because I was in Paris with the only man I'd ever loved.

I felt fluttery and twitchy. I didn't know if it was fear or desire. Either way, there was no turning back. I was with Bryan, wherever we were going. I didn't feel guilty, I didn't feel naughty, I didn't feel wrong. I stepped into our future as I broke the kiss. "Take me to your hotel room."

I'd never in my life seen a man hail a cab so fast.

* * *

The taxi slowed down for a light on the rue de Rivoli. I peered ahead, noting the clogged street in front of us, the boulevard packed with cars. Since we wouldn't reach the W for another ten minutes at this rate, I closed the scratched-up partition that separated us from the driver.

"It's like you can read my mind," Bryan said, and returned for a deeper kiss, kissing me until the taxi pulled up to the hotel, and he handed several bills to the driver. He made a brief stop at the front desk, and then we stepped into a waiting elevator. As the doors closed, he placed his hand on the small of my back. We made it to the fourth floor, down the hall, and to his room. He slid the card key in the door, and once inside, I tore off my coat, and he tossed off his jacket.

His room was heavenly, with a gorgeous gilded mirror and antique nightstands. French windows, fittingly, led to a balcony. But I had little interest in the surroundings when there was a king-size bed with a soft white down comforter that called my name. I longed to be naked on it with my legs wrapped around Bryan.

He stood behind me and ran his hands along my arms. He reached my hands, clasping my fingers in his, and whispered in my ear, "Do you have any idea how much I want to make love to you right now?"

"How much?"

"More than I have ever wanted anything before." He swept my hair from my neck and kissed me there, sending tingles of insane pleasure down my spine. I understood the word "swoon" in a whole new way. He walked me to the bed and laid me down, then pulled off my boots. He ran his hands up the inside of my legs. Every touch thrilled me. Every second of contact sent me higher.

"You have far too many clothes on, Kat."

"Take them off. Take them all off."

He unzipped my skirt and gently removed it, placing it on the nearby chair. My sweater was next, and he groaned when he saw me in only my bra and panties. Then it was my turn. I sat up and unknotted his tie then began on his shirt, enjoying the release of each button as I trailed my hands down the white T-shirt underneath. One shirt came off, then the other, and I pulled back to admire him. His chest was broad and sturdy, his stomach flat and cut. I ran my teeth over my bottom lip as I looked down at his pants, at how turned on he was.

He unhooked my bra and touched my breasts and somehow made me even hotter for him. He kneeled to strip off my underwear, then kissed my ankle and traced a line up my calf to behind my knee. My insides were on fire. My body was aflame. He pressed a palm gently against my belly, guiding me back onto the bed.

"You're so beautiful," he murmured as he returned to my thighs, grazing his tongue between my legs, tasting my desire for him.

I gasped in pleasure and arched against him as he traced long, soft, lingering lines up and down.

"It's better than I ever dreamed," I whispered between ragged breaths as I grabbed at his soft, thick hair. His firm hands hugged my thighs, and he made a sound like I was the sweetest thing he'd ever tasted.

The way he moved his tongue, the way his lips kissed me, made me believe nothing else existed. This pleasure was all there was, it was all I felt, all I wanted —to be spread open to him, to have his mouth devouring me, to say his name, and then to cry out in crazy ecstasy. Nothing could ever be better than this.

He moved up, and I was tipsy, buzzed from the most delicious drink ever—the way he knew me, the way the secret treasure map to my body had been his to follow. He looked satisfied with his work as he began to unbuckle his pants. I sat up to help, dying to see him fully naked. He stepped back from the bed, letting his pants fall to the floor, then I pulled down his boxer briefs. God, he was beautiful, carved and hard as steel. My hand had a mind of its own. He pressed his teeth against his lip and cursed quietly in pleasured agony as I touched him.

Then he reached for a condom.

He hovered over me and teased me with his kisses, keeping me on my back, brushing his lips across my lips, my cheeks, my eyelids, even the tip of my nose. Even that felt good from him. Everything felt good with Bryan. I sighed as he kissed my neck and then threaded his fingers through my hair, pulling me close.

"Tell me what you want, Kat. I want to hear you say it."

"I want you to make love to me."

I'd never said "make love" to anyone before. Bryan was the only person I'd ever loved, and I'd never been with him like this. The way it seemed on the silver screen, with the big love of your life. When young love and passion turn to smoldering tenderness in the sheets. The waiting, the wanting, the longing, as bodies come together skin against skin, nothing held back, no distance, no time, no pretending. It had always seemed so perfect, so epic, so out of this world.

Now, here I was, feeling more than I'd ever imagined.

I placed my hands on his firm, toned chest, tracing his skin, his muscles, searing them into my memory now that I finally could, now that I finally knew what he felt like. He parted my legs and entered me, and I moaned as he filled me. Who said it was supposed to feel this good? But it did. Beyond any and all reason.

"You," he said softly, looking at me. "You."

He buried himself in me, and I was in another world, in another time. I was drowning in pleasure, swallowed whole by desire. I was all the air I'd ever breathed. I was the edge of reason, and nothing else existed but the feeling of him moving deep inside of me, his body touching mine at last. Heat rose in my chest, a fire radiating from my center to the tips of my fingers, the far reaches of my eyelashes, and through to the inside and out of my heart, as if it might burst with all the feelings—love, lust, want, and then, most of all, ecstatic and utter happiness. Completeness. Allness. I was lost, and then I was found, and I was suddenly aware of every sensation in my body. Of how he placed a hand on my hip, how his breath tasted good, how the soft little never-shaven hairs on the backs of my thighs stood on end. I'd gone to heaven still alive, and everything felt ravishing as he plunged into me, gripped my wrists, and brought me there again.

And when it ended, when we lay sated in bed, I outlined his body with my fingertips, planting little kisses across the hard planes of his belly, the firm muscles of his arms, the breadth of his chest that felt like home. We were silent for another moment, then I felt his hand slip into mine.

It was the laughter, it was the movies, it was Paris. It was the hero holding a boom box in the rain. I had always wanted to believe I could have love like in the movies. Now, I knew I could. It wasn't just Hollywood.

I could have this man for the rest of my life and never want for anything more.

32

KAT

Present Day

"Something isn't working."

Charms and trinkets were spread out on the tray table. I'd aligned them along one of the silver chains I always kept with me. But they didn't look right. I thought of my mom setting up displays in her store. She'd arrange some picture frames, then mugs, then perhaps a bracelet or two. Inevitably, she took one away.

"It's what Coco Chanel has always said: 'Before you leave the house, look in the mirror and take one thing off,'" my mother had said to me, quoting the fashion icon.

Bryan looked up from the book he was reading on his tablet. We were on the same flight home, and he'd used miles again to upgrade me.

"There's too much going on," I said. "It needs to be simpler."

He grinned and returned to his book. I liked that we could talk constantly or not at all.

Playing around with the design a bit more, I narrowed down the piece to a star, a key, and a sun. I tapped him on the shoulder.

"I like it better. The question is, when you get this big order from Elizabeth's, how are you going to make them all?"

"Yeah. There is that." I'd been so focused on the designs and assembling the perfect prototype that I hadn't started to address the nuts and bolts. Soon, I'd have to. "I've always just made them myself."

"You could keep doing that. If there were ten or twenty of you and several machines to help out as well."

"Oh, haha."

"No, I'm serious. You can't be boutique and bespoke much longer, Kat."

"I have to land the deal first." I moved a star trinket to another position on the strand. But it still didn't look right. "Crap."

Bryan placed his hand gently on mine. "Hey."

My agitation started to fade with his touch.

"You know, Kat. I happen to know this guy who runs a similar business. Makes gift items. Some hand-crafted, some machine-assisted. The products get rave reviews, and the business is growing like crazy. He knows how to manufacture something at scale and make sure it's still beautiful and has a personal touch.

Perhaps I could see if he'd be willing to accommodate your new line of necklaces at his factory?"

I looked at him, wide-eyed and open-jawed. "You'd do that? How much would it cost me?"

He laughed. "First of all, of course I'd do it. Second, don't worry about the cost."

"You can't just give me something for free because . . ." I let my voice trail off.

"Because? Because we're back to not seeing each other for another four weeks after we land in"—he looked at his watch—"three hours?"

"Not that."

He put the tip of his index finger on the star trinket and pushed the star aside. He moved the other charms too. Then he pushed the mini skeleton key to the center of the chain.

"Not for free. I have a proposition for you."

He told me his idea.

I nodded appreciatively. "That's not a bad idea."

* * *

Bryan grabbed my suitcases from the luggage carousel.

"So, I'll see you in a month."

"So, this is it."

We'd decided not to share a car back into Manhattan. That would be too tempting. He reached out to give me a hug, and I moved in close to him, lingering in the crook of his neck, wishing I could smother him in kisses and go home with him and do more than kiss. Do everything, again and again, all night long. Then, I spotted someone I knew at the next carousel. A dapper man. A sharp-dressed woman. Waiting for luggage.

No way.

There was no way my professor and his wife were here at the same time. But she'd said they were going on a trip. Theirs was an international flight as well.

Bryan wrapped me in a warm embrace, but I didn't feel reassured. I'd gone too far, and I knew it. I could see my world crashing around me, all the things I'd worked hard for breaking into pieces at my feet. I wasn't supposed to get caught.

No hanky-panky or else an F.

Then, the professor turned, and he wasn't my professor after all. He was just a man who looked like him.

I relaxed momentarily.

But later that night, as I worked on my designs for Claire using the curved-nose pliers on a key, I didn't feel like I'd just returned home from a romantic trip to Paris. I didn't feel like I was such a smart businesswoman. I felt like someone trying to get away with trickery. Someone trying to pull the wool over shareholders' eyes, to fool the public, to get off scot-free.

Like a liar.

That's precisely who I was now.

But that wasn't me. That wasn't who I wanted to be.

I had a choice. I had my future in front of me. It

had to be a future I could live with. I had to be the *me* I could live with.

My stomach twisted into knots, and I took a deep breath as I knocked on my professor's door. It was open, and he was waiting for me. I'd called earlier to request the meeting to ensure I wouldn't back down before I arrived.

He gestured for me to come in. My boots clacked loudly on the tiled floor of the office.

"Have a seat, Ms. Harper. Good to see you. I trust you had a productive time in Paris?"

"I did. It was a great trip."

"Fantastic. And how is everything going this semester with Made Here? We only have a few more weeks left, but the reports have been good. I'm pleased."

I gathered up all my courage. My shoulders rose and fell, and then I began. "I wanted to let you know that during the course of the semester and my time at Made Here, I have fallen in love with Bryan Leighton. Well, I suppose you could say I've fallen deeper in love, because I was already in love with him five years ago and never stopped."

Professor Oliver looked at me quizzically and narrowed his eyebrows. "I'm sorry. I don't understand."

I steeled myself to say the words without tripping on them. I was clinical and businesslike as I laid my confession bare. "I was involved with him when I was younger, and I'm also involved with him now. I could tell you that we tried to stop. That we tried to wait until the mentorship was over. I could tell you how important this class is to me. I could tell you how badly I want to graduate. I could tell you how much Bryan values his company's relationship with the school. Those would all be true. But what's also true is that I broke your rule about being involved with my mentor. And because of that, I don't think he should be my mentor anymore."

He nodded several times with pursed lips that formed a scowl. "I see."

He picked up a pencil from his desk and began twirling it. Thumb to forefinger. Thumb to forefinger. After several perfectly executed twirls, he put the pencil down and looked at me.

"It would seem you have a problem, then, Ms. Harper. You no longer have a mentor. Without a mentor, you cannot pass this class. Without this class, you cannot graduate."

* * *

Claire adored my designs. They exceeded her expectations, she declared over espresso and chocolate biscuits. But her admiration was a Pyrrhic victory. She'd detailed the conditions of her investment, and I'd made a conscious choice to violate them. I wouldn't be able to finish my degree, and that broke the deal.

She held up the slim silver chain with the vintage key on it, shaking her head with pride. We were at a café on the Upper East Side. "This? Yes. I can tell you right now Elizabeth's will carry it."

I gave her a curious look. How could she make such a guarantee? But it didn't matter. She could say all she wanted about Elizabeth's, but she'd be taking it all back when I broke the news.

"I'm glad you like it. Really, truly, I am. But there's a problem," I said, and then told her everything, including how her husband had the no hanky-panky warning posted on his website.

She cackled when she heard that. "I had no idea. Really? It says no hanky-panky?"

I grabbed my phone and tapped in his URL, showing her the screen.

She laughed even harder. "He's one to talk."

"What do you mean?"

"I was his student. He's such a hypocrite."

"Really?"

Even as my future with her circled the drain, I couldn't help but join her in peals of laughter that echoed around the café. The couple at the table next to us peered over.

"You were his student?"

"Yes. I wasn't even his protégé. I was his actual student fifteen years ago when I went to NYU and he was teaching management skills. Some management skills. He fell in love with his student while he was teaching her. For him to post that about no hanky-panky is incredibly amusing. But those are his rules. And I respect them. And you must abide."

I nodded, a heaviness in my chest. I would have liked doing business with her, but I would have to go it alone. I'd have to start over in my quest to help my parents. I pushed my chair away from the table, stood up, and offered her a hand to shake.

She waved me off. "This is what you've learned at business school? This is what you've learned from me?"

"What do you mean?"

"You're just going to give up?"

"You made your stipulations pretty clear, Mrs. Oliver. And I respect them. I am so, so grateful that you were willing to take a chance on me and my work, but I let you down. I'm not going to be able to finish this class. Or work with you."

She pointed to my chair. "Sit back down."

Her voice was commanding, imperious, even. I immediately followed her order.

"In business school, did you learn that there is more than one way to solve a business problem?"

"Sure."

"And would you say you have a business problem?"

"I suppose you could say that."

"Then, think about another way around this. Think about what you need, truly need, to finish your experiential learning class."

I needed a rewind button. Better tunnel vision. Self-restraint.

She kept speaking. "You need a mentor." She

waved a bejeweled hand airily. I bet she could cut a glass door off in seconds with the size of that ring.

"But that's the problem, Mrs. Oliver. I don't have a mentor anymore."

She gestured to herself. "Am I chopped liver?"

I flinched in surprise. "What?" It came out like a stutter.

"I'd like to think I've been somewhat instrumental in your hands-on business learning this semester."

I leaned forward, still not sure if she was truly serious, or if I could even pull this off. The class called for us to be paired with business leaders who ran actual companies. She seemed more of a benefactor, a generous angel investor. "You would do that, Mrs. Oliver? I mean, Claire."

She took a sip of her espresso. "You can call me Claire. But I have another name as well. I don't go by it often, and I don't really let many people know my other name. But the reason I am sure we can get these designs into Elizabeth's stores is because I am Elizabeth Mortimer, and as the head of Elizabeth's, I would be delighted to finish out the semester as your mentor."

Fairy godmother, I'd say.

* * *

I raced back to NYU. The cab pulled up to the curb, and I thrust several dollars into the driver's hand and pushed hard on the door. I ran up the marble steps to Professor Oliver's office. He still had office hours now and was finishing up with another student.

I paced as I waited for the guy to leave. I reviewed my speech in my head, still marveling that Claire Oliver was Elizabeth Mortimer, head of the luxury department store chain that wanted to carry my designs. There was only one obstacle in the way—her husband.

The other student left, and I rushed to the door, then knocked.

"Hello again, Ms. Harper."

He gestured to the same chair I'd sat in hours ago.

"If you've come to convince me to bend the rules, I should warn you, I'm not known for my mercy." He spoke the last words with a smile on his face, but he was deadly serious. His kind manner could never be mistaken for leniency.

I shook my head. "I wouldn't ask you to do that. Instead, I wanted to present a different solution. You said I needed a mentor to pass this class. Mentors are business leaders who are alumni. I don't have one now, but I've been working closely this semester with a businesswoman named Elizabeth Mortimer. You might know her. She runs the Elizabeth's stores. And via that relationship, I have gained two rounds of seed funding, an investment to fund design research, and a distribution deal in those department stores. Ms. Mortimer has guided me on design stylings, as well as offered insight into the best direction for my business."

"Elizabeth Mortimer, you say?" He seemed amused.

"Yes. She is a very sharp businesswoman."

"So I've heard. And it sounds like she has indeed been influential in your growth and development, Ms. Harper. But part of the requirement for the class is that the protégés help the business leaders solve real-world business challenges. How have you done that?" His normally chipper voice was laced with skepticism.

I thought of the conversation a few weeks ago when Claire, aka Elizabeth, had first presented the opportunity. "The Elizabeth's stores need a jewelry line to focus their holiday marketing around. Elizabeth had been looking for a new style that would draw attention. She loved the designs I brought back from Paris. I've also been able to line up a manufacturing partner to have them produced in time. It'll be a fast turnaround, but we can pull it off, and with her marketing and with my manufacturer's savvy, I think we will have not only solved the business problems, but also provided an answer to the age-old question at holiday time: 'What do I buy for the woman I love?'"

Professor Oliver pursed his lips and nodded a few times. "And Ms. Mortimer is open to this?"

I found it odd that we were discussing Ms. Mortimer as if she were not his wife. I supposed that was in keeping with her veiled identity though. She wanted to be both Mrs. Claire Oliver and Ms. Elizabeth Mortimer.

"Yes. She would be willing to step in officially as

my mentor for the rest of the term. I will have had Bryan Leighton for the first few months, and Ms. Mortimer to finish out the term. And to be quite honest, that seems rather fitting for my business. Both have helped me tremendously to grow and expand My Favorite Mistakes. And I have, in turn, helped both of their businesses, as you know from the reports."

He removed his glasses, picked up a white cloth from his desk, and cleaned the lenses. When the glasses were free of fingerprints, he put them back on. "Ms. Harper, has anyone ever told you that you're not too shabby at negotiation?" He cracked a grin and extended his hand. "Welcome back. I trust there will be no hanky-panky with Ms. Mortimer as you finish out the term?"

"None, sir."

"Good. I do have a suggestion now for your business. Perhaps it's time to move beyond the name My Favorite Mistakes, since your business is moving beyond that idea."

"What do you think would be a good name?"

"Seeing as I suspect you have a rather bright future in front of you as a jewelry designer, I would suggest a simple name. I would suggest your name. That is what all the fashion icons do. I think your customers will soon want to give, and to wear, Kat Harper necklaces."

I smiled. "It has a nice ring to it."

EPILOGUE

Bryan

Present Day

"Close your eyes."

I pressed my palms over her eyes as we reached the block with her parents' store.

"Maybe you'd like to blindfold me?" she teased. And that was not a bad idea.

"I'll do that later, don't you worry," I said.

"Oh, I wasn't worried."

"Just keep them closed."

"I can't see a thing. Don't let me trip," she said.

"I won't." I would never let anything happen to my Kat. I was so damn lucky to have her back. To have her be mine at last. Part of me couldn't believe I'd been so foolish to give her up, but I also knew I had to. I knew we'd never have worked then. But now? We worked so damn well.

And I knew it was meant to be.

I guided her along the sidewalk. The sea air reminded me of long, lazy summer days here in Mystic five years ago. It reminded me of summer nights spent falling in love. Right now, with the start of December upon us, the air smelled of pine and freshly falling snow. A few flakes drifted from the darkening afternoon sky, promising a night by a warm fire and blankets of white in the morning.

Kat graduated two days ago. There was little fanfare—she simply finished her exams, checked her grades online, and verified that she had, in fact, attained her MBA.

I wasn't the first person she told. First, she'd called Claire—Kat said she now thought of her as a super-hero with a secret identity.

Kat's necklaces were faring well the first week in Claire's stores. The My Favorite Mistakes line was still selling online and in boutiques, but the Eliza-beth's customers favored her simpler styles. Rather than a star, a key, and a sunburst jammed on one necklace, they were opting for single pendants and embracing the European look of the charms, fresh from the markets of Paris. Of course, there were shoppers with quirkier tastes, and for those, the cat and dog charms appealed. Still others liked the cameos and brooches.

"Be charmed with a Kat Harper necklace."

That was the new tagline.

I was so proud of her. Her business was growing, and in a few weeks, she planned to pay off her parents' loan from the revenue.

"Almost there."

She held her hands over mine, purple mittens looking so damn adorable on her. We passed the café. The bell on the door jingled when someone came out, and the telltale scent of coffee trailed behind.

"Here we are," I said, taking my hands off her eyes.

She stumbled at the sight, and I grabbed her elbow to keep her from slipping. Then I watched with satisfaction as she took in the view.

Mystic Landing hadn't only been transformed for the holidays—it had been totally transformed. A makeover and a face-lift. There was a new sign made out of brushed metal, window displays that married a sleek and retro design, and a glass door that had been spruced up, with the name of the store painted in Kat's favorite color—purple.

I held open the door, smiling as I watched her wander inside, mesmerized by the changes, her eyes the size of saucers. The old beige Berber rug had been replaced by a warm cranberry carpet. The standard wooden shelves and displays had been removed, and instead, the frames and mugs, the books and cards, the vases and other gifts for sale were displayed on high and low wooden tables, some modern, some antique. The perfect mix of old rustic charm that had made this place a centerpiece of the town for many years carried over and a new twist to send the store into the future.

The kitschier items had been banished. In their place were classier wares: small pitchers in brushed metal, a cute pink pot for making sauces, wineglasses with clever patterns on them.

My favorite display was the his-and-hers gift set, courtesy of Made Here and Kat Harper—a vintage key necklace coupled with a set of cuff links fashioned from the padlocks kept in storage from the lover's bridge in Paris.

Kat and I were a good pair at a lot of things, including business partnerships. The chance to market this line of gifts together was my proposition —that was all I wanted when I said she could make her necklaces at my factory, knowing it was too good an offer to pass up.

Her parents waved to her, but neither one of them rushed over. They were too busy ringing up customers, and I knew that that made Kat unbelievably happy. I'd always had a hunch that there was another solution to the store's woes.

She turned to me, her eyes shining with happiness. "Is my jaw on the floor right now?"

"Something like that." I grinned big and wide.

"Did you do this?"

My answer was a sheepish shrug.

"But how? I knew you'd been out to visit the store and check on things. You told me you were helping my parents figure out some new inventory plans. But this?"

Pride suffused me. I'd done this. I wanted to, but I had to. I had to show her how much she meant to me. I knew this was the way. "That's what I was up to. It was a surprise. For you."

"You did all this?"

I nodded.

"They let you? My parents are stoic about taking help from me," she whispered. "I couldn't imagine they'd accept it from you, even if you're their daughter's boyfriend."

Another smile. "They did."

"But how did you convince them?"

"I told them I wanted to do it as a gift to you."

"And that was all it took?" She eyed me skeptically.

"Sort of," I said.

There was a lull in the action at the counter and her parents came over, giving a round of quick hugs. Her dad clapped me on the back.

"The floor is yours," Kat's father said, and took a step back, putting his arm around Kat's mom, giving me space.

"What is it?" Kat asked.

It was everything I'd ever wanted. She was everything to me, and I didn't want to ever be without her.

I was ready, and I hoped she'd say yes.

"It's really daunting being in love with a jewelry designer," I said. "You can't really get her a necklace or earrings or even a ring to show your love, because chances are, she has her own ideas in those areas and might be a little particular. So this"—I spread out my arms to indicate the revitalization of the store—"is my gift to you. But it's more like a promise. It's a promise that I don't want to be your favorite mistake. That I want to be your forever mistake, if you'll have me."

* * *

Kat

My heart stopped for a moment, and I couldn't move or form words.

"What I'm really trying to say is I don't ever want to lose you again. Now that I have you, I want to be with you always. Will you be mine?"

He bent down on one knee, and my heart nearly stopped. But then he reached for his wallet. I raised an eyebrow curiously as I watched. He removed a tiny white bag that looked familiar.

"You might remember the day I bought this. Back at a little shop in the Village with you. I've kept it since then. In my wallet, in this bag, for more than five years. I got it for you then and planned to give it to you as a promise. It's just a little thing, but you'd said you always loved Paris."

He reached into the bag and handed me a ring I did remember looking at in the little shop. A little fleur-de-lis in tiny purple stones, and it looked like it had been carried in a wallet for five years. Which is to say, it looked beautiful.

"You kept this all that time?" I wondered.

"With me every single day. Kat, it's always been you for me. Always."

I grabbed his hand and pulled him to me, wrapping my arms around him.

"I'll buy you a real ring," he said. "But I want you to design it, okay?"

I nodded.

"So, that's a yes?"

Rays of happiness burst from my chest. "I'm yours. I always have been. I always will be."

Then I kissed him, and of all our wonderful kisses, this kiss was the very best of all. Because it was a new beginning. Here in my home away from home, in the town where I grew up, we'd come back to each other. We had each other to hold tight and never let go.

* * *

Be sure to grab the next book in this series — The Private Rehearsal. It's FREE in KU and you won't be resist this sexy forbidden romance!

Binge the entire Caught Up In Love Series FREE in KU!
The Pretending Plot: Reeve and Sutton's fake fiancé romance
The Dating Proposal: Chris and McKenna's dating makeover/workplace romance
The Second Chance Plan: Bryan and Kat's second chance office romance

The Private Rehearsal: Davis and Jill's forbidden
romance

Are you curious about Elise's story? Dive into the
sinfully   sexy   romance   marriage-of-convenience
romance Part-Time Lover, FREE IN KU!

BE A LOVELY

Want to be the first to know of sales, new releases, special deals and giveaways? Sign up for my newsletter today!

Want to be part of a fun, feel-good place to talk about books and romance, and get sneak peeks of covers and advance copies of my books? Be a Lovely!

ACKNOWLEDGMENTS

Thanks to Rosemary!

MORE BOOKS BY LAUREN

I've written more than 100 books! **All of these titles below are FREE in Kindle Unlimited**!

Double Pucked

A sexy, outrageous MFM hockey romantic comedy!

Puck Yes

A fake marriage, spicy MFM hockey rom com!

The Virgin Society Series

Meet the Virgin Society – great friends who'd do anything for each other. Indulge in these forbidden, emotionally-charged, and wildly sexy age-gap romances!

The RSVP

The Tryst

The Tease

The Dating Games Series

A fun, sexy romantic comedy series about friends in the city and their dating mishaps!

The Virgin Next Door

Two A Day

The Good Guy Challenge

How To Date Series (New and ongoing)

Four great friends. Four chances to learn how to date

again. Four standalone romantic comedies full of love, sex and meet-cute shenanigans.

My So-Called Sex Life

Plays Well With Others

A romantic comedy adventure/romantic suspense standalone

A Real Good Bad Thing

Boyfriend Material

Four fabulous heroines. Four outrageous proposals. Four chances at love in this sexy rom-com series!

Asking For a Friend

Sex and Other Shiny Objects

One Night Stand-In

Overnight Service

Big Rock Series

My #1 New York Times Bestselling sexy as sin, irreverent, male-POV romantic comedy!

Big Rock

Mister O

Well Hung

Full Package

Joy Ride

Hard Wood

Happy Endings Series

Romance starts with a bang in this series of standalones

following a group of friends seeking and avoiding love!

Come Again

Shut Up and Kiss Me

Kismet

My Single-Versary

Ballers And Babes

Sexy sports romance standalones guaranteed to make
you hot!

Most Valuable Playboy

Most Likely to Score

A Wild Card Kiss

Rules of Love Series

Athlete, virgins and weddings!

The Virgin Rule Book

The Virgin Game Plan

The Virgin Replay

The Virgin Scorecard

The Extravagant Series

Bodyguards, billionaires and hoteliers in this sexy, high-
stakes series of standalones!

One Night Only

One Exquisite Touch

My One-Week Husband

The Guys Who Got Away Series

Friends in New York City and California fall in love in this fun and hot rom-com series!

Birthday Suit

Dear Sexy Ex-Boyfriend

The What If Guy

Thanks for Last Night

The Dream Guy Next Door

Always Satisfied Series

A group of friends in New York City find love and laughter
in this series of sexy standalones!

Satisfaction Guaranteed

Never Have I Ever

Instant Gratification

PS It's Always Been You

The Gift Series

An after dark series of standalones! Explore your fantasies!

The Engagement Gift

The Virgin Gift

The Decadent Gift

The Heartbreakers Series

Three brothers. Three rockers. Three standalone sexy
romantic comedies.

Once Upon a Real Good Time

Once Upon a Sure Thing

Once Upon a Wild Fling

Sinful Men

A high-stakes, high-octane, sexy-as-sin romantic suspense series!

My Sinful Nights

My Sinful Desire

My Sinful Longing

My Sinful Love

My Sinful Temptation

From Paris With Love

Swoony, sweeping romances set in Paris!

Wanderlust

Part-Time Lover

One Love Series

A group of friends in New York falls in love one by one in this sexy rom-com series!

The Sexy One

The Hot One

The Knocked Up Plan

Come As You Are

Lucky In Love Series

A small town romance full of heat and blue collar heroes and sexy heroines!

Best Laid Plans

The Feel Good Factor

Nobody Does It Better

Unzipped

No Regrets

An angsty, sexy, emotional, new adult trilogy about one young couple fighting to break free of their pasts!

The Start of Us

The Thrill of It

Every Second With You

The Caught Up in Love Series

A group of friends finds love!

The Pretending Plot

The Dating Proposal

The Second Chance Plan

The Private Rehearsal

Seductive Nights Series

A high heat series full of danger and spice!

Night After Night

After This Night

One More Night

A Wildly Seductive Night

Joy Delivered Duet

A high-heat, wickedly sexy series of standalones that will set your sheets on fire!

Nights With Him

Forbidden Nights

Unbreak My Heart

A standalone second chance emotional roller coaster of a

romance

The Muse

A magical realism romance set in Paris

Good Love Series of sexy rom-coms co-written with Lili Valente!

I also write MM romance under the name L. Blakely!

Hopelessly Bromantic Duet (MM)

Roomies to lovers to enemies to fake boyfriends

Hopelessly Bromantic

Here Comes My Man

Men of Summer Series (MM)

Two baseball players on the same team fall in love in a forbidden romance spanning five epic years

Scoring With Him

Winning With Him

All In With Him

MM Standalone Novels

A Guy Walks Into My Bar

The Bromance Zone

One Time Only

The Best Men (Co-written with Sarina Bowen)

Winner Takes All Series (MM)

A series of emotionally-charged and irresistibly sexy

standalone MM sports romances!

The Boyfriend Comeback

Turn Me On

A Very Filthy Game

Limited Edition Husband

Manhandled

If you want a personalized recommendation, email me at
laurenblakelybooks@gmail.com!

CONTACT

I love hearing from readers! You can find me on TikTok at LaurenBlakelyBooks, Instagram at LaurenBlakelyBooks, Facebook at LaurenBlakelyBooks, or online at LaurenBlakely.com. You can also email me at laurenblakelybooks@ gmail.com

Made in the USA
Coppell, TX
04 May 2024

32029281R00144